P9-CDW-877

A Filly for Melinda

ALSO BY DORIS GATES

Blue Willow
Little Vic
Lord of the Sky: Zeus
The Warrior Goddess: Athena
The Golden God: Apollo
Two Queens of Heaven: Aphrodite and Demeter
Mightiest of Mortals: Heracles
A Fair Wind for Troy
A Morgan for Melinda

A Filly for Melinda

a novel by DORIS GATES

The Viking Press
New York

HARDEMAN COUNTY LIBRARY
QUANAH, TEXAS

First Edition
Copyright © 1984 by Doris Gates
All rights reserved
First published in 1984 by The Viking Press
40 West 23rd Street, New York, New York 10010
Published simultaneously in Canada by Penguin Books Canada Limited
Printed in U.S.A.
1   2   3   4   5   88   87   86   85   84

Library of Congress Cataloging in Publication Data
Gates, Doris, date.   A filly for Melinda.
Sequel to: A Morgan for Melinda.
Summary: Twelve-year-old Melinda faces the difficult
choice between keeping her beloved filly, Littly Missy,
or helping her parents through a family crisis.
[1. Horses—Fiction]   I. Title
PZ7.G216Fi 1984   [Fic]   83-14617   ISBN 0-670-31328-9

For my goddaughter Mariam Gates Wheeler,
whose father got The Cat

Contents

A Filly for Melinda

1

Arrival

I'll never know what woke me up that morning. Dad had warned me before I went to bed that the foal might arrive during the night. Merry Jo had shown definite signs of an approaching birth. So I suppose I had it on my mind when I went to sleep.

Before I really knew I was awake, I was sitting up in bed and looking out the dark window. This was only the end of January, and dawn was still a long way off. My upstairs window looks out across the backyard to the barn and riding ring. I got out of bed and padded across the cold board floor to the window and looked out. There was no moon, but the stars were bright.

You could just make out the shape of things outside.

I switched on the bedroom light and hurried into my clothes. As I reached for my imitation sheepskin coat, Fancy, my white whippet, came out of her bed. She follows me everywhere, and she wasn't about to have me go out into the dark without her. I took up the battery lantern I had placed beside my bed last evening, just in case, and the two of us headed toward the barn.

The lantern gave a good strong light. I saw that Ethan, my Morgan gelding, was standing quietly in the paddock next to the barn. I slid open the barn door outside the paddock. Fancy tried to follow me, but I made her go back, then shut the door in her face. The last thing Merry Jo needed right now was a lively little dog frisking around her.

When I got to Merry Jo's stall, I called her name and quietly slid back the stall door. She was lying in the deep straw covering the floor of the stall, wall to wall. One quick look made me pretty sure her baby was coming. The mare was breathing hard and seemed restless, though she was lying down. She kept moving her head from side to side, and every now and then she would put out her front feet as if she were going to get up. Then she would lie back again.

I set the lantern down and went slowly up to her. She nickered as I approached. I smoothed her neck, and it felt damp.

Merry Jo is a grand champion Morgan, thirteen years old. This was her first baby, and I was mighty anxious for things to go right. I turned to leave the stall and get Dad. He knows all there is to know about horses, for someone who isn't a vet. I wanted him here.

But then, suddenly, Merry Jo laid her head down and stretched out flat, her four feet stiff in front of her body. Her tail, braided and wrapped, was flung up. I knew this was it.

I had never seen a foal or any other animal born before. But I had been given the books on Morgans and horse culture that Missy had collected, and I had read them all. I knew quite a bit. (Missy, in case you don't know, was the old lady who owned Merry Jo. She died about a year ago and willed Merry Jo to me. The mare, of course, was already in foal then.) I knew there wasn't time to go and get Dad if I wanted to see this foal born, and I did want to see it. There would be time to call him if things weren't going right. I set the lantern down where its light wouldn't bother the mare, and drew close to her flanks. They were quivering slightly. As I watched, a tiny hoof came slowly out of the mare's body. It was wrapped in a transparent covering, which I knew was the birth sac. So far, so good. In seconds another hoof appeared, then a little nose resting on a foreleg. Things were going all right. This was the way a foal should come: forefeet first and nose resting on them. I reached over and took hold of the thin membrane in order to break it so the foal could breathe. It was surprisingly tough, but I managed finally.

Nothing more happened for a little while, then Merry Jo's body drew up in a kind of spasm and a little shoulder appeared. The foal was coming on a kind of slant from inside its mother's body—Nature's way of making the birth easier. The other shoulder followed quickly. Again mare and baby rested for a bit. Then, amazingly quickly, the rest of the foal slid out onto the straw. I folded the birth sac back from its body, careful not to break the umbilical cord, which was still pumping blood into the newborn foal. I could feel it throbbing. Merry Jo lay quietly, and I moved the foal carefully up against her so she could feel it and know that it was there. It felt wet, and it looked wet and dark and hardly alive. I was surprised at how tiny it was, never having seen a brand-new foal before. It was hardly as big as Fancy, but with longer legs.

I don't know when I've felt so thrilled. At the same time I wanted to cry. It was all so wonderful. Here, after eleven months in its mother's body, was a little new thing that hadn't been part of earth even fifteen minutes ago. Merry Jo's new baby.

A voice sounded behind me, low and pleased. "So it's here, is it?" Dad said.

I looked up at him, very glad he was there because I wasn't too sure what should be done next.

The birth sac was still attached to the foal's umbilical cord.

"Have you got a colt or a filly?"

I had forgotten to notice! But what went through my mind just then was that most fathers would have said, "What have *we* got?" Dad was remembering that Merry Jo was my mare and so was her foal. He's like that. Very fair.

He lifted the little body to its feet. "You have a filly, Melinda, by all that's wonderful! Hello, Little Missy. Welcome to this world."

I had already decided to name it "Little Missy" if the foal was a filly, because "Missy" was the name I gave the old lady who had willed Merry Jo to me. It was a nickname, but she liked it better than her own, so that's what we three called her, Dad and Mom and I.

The foal stood unsteadily on its little feet, which didn't look like hooves at all but like layers of thin horn placed one on top of another, the front and sides all scraggly. "Feathers," they are called. The birth sac had dropped from its body and now trailed in the straw.

Dad got to his feet. "I'll get the iodine and some towels. Try to keep them both quiet. I won't be a minute."

Our tack is kept in the empty stall right next to Merry Jo's, so it was only half a minute before he was back with the iodine and towels I had set out yesterday afternoon.

During that half minute the umbilical cord had separated itself from the birth sac, and I was supporting the foal with my two hands so it couldn't lie down before Dad had soaked the cord with iodine to prevent infection. That's very important.

He did this first, then rubbed her vigorously with the clean old bath towels. Next he gathered Little Missy into his hands and placed her in front of Merry Jo. The mare nuzzled her gently. Then Dad squatted down near the mare's tail.

"Move the lantern closer," he said.

Quite a lot of wet, slippery-looking stuff was hanging out of Merry Jo where the foal had emerged. Now Dad took it all up in his two hands and knotted it.

"Now she can't step on it when she gets to her feet and pull the afterbirth out of her before it's ready to come."

"When will that be?" I asked.

"Within an hour if all goes well." He picked up the lantern and signaled me toward the stall door. The mare and her foal were still quietly resting in the straw.

"We must leave them now," he told me. "The mare must be left alone to get onto her feet when she's ready. And the foal must be allowed to find her nipples without anyone around to distract it. How about some breakfast?"

"What time is it?" I asked.

He put a hand down near the lantern light. "Almost six o'clock. We'll put a call in to Dr. Vance so he can come out and check Merry Jo and the baby as soon as possible."

"But everything's all right, isn't it?"

"As far as I can tell, it is. But he'll want to give them each a tetanus shot, and I want to be sure that all the afterbirth comes out."

"How can he tell?"

"By looking at it," Dad said. "Within the next hour I'll go out and check, and if the afterbirth has come, I'll put it in a bucket and keep it safe so he can spread it out and know if it's all there."

As I have said, it was near the end of January, and though spring had started to come to the Carmel Valley, it was still pitch-dark at six in the morning. Dad is a rural mail carrier, and ordinarily he would have been at the post office in Carmel by this time. But since this was Saturday, both he and I could be home. Mom works at an architect's office in Carmel. Right now she was upstairs asleep. None of us get up much before eight on Saturdays. But this morning was different.

We entered the screened porch of this old-fashioned ranch house. Toro Estates, the subdivision where we live, used to be a cattle ranch, and our house is the old ranch house. We're high in the hills above the Carmel

Valley. It's a steep climb to our house from the valley highway. Across from our house, which is the last one on the road, are wide meadows and hills beyond. You can ride on good trails all the way from our place almost to Salinas. And once, before Merry Jo was bred, Dad and I did just that. He rode Merry Jo and I rode Ethan. Missy was visiting her publishers in New York at the time. She wrote mystery stories and encouraged me to write a book about my learning how to be a horse-woman. What I am writing now I am adding to that book.

We went into the kitchen, and Dad switched on the light.

"Don't wake up your mother," he cautioned me.

It surprised me that he said that. I'm not one to go banging around, and I understood perfectly that she wanted to sleep late on Saturdays. I guess he saw something like resentment on my face.

He grinned and looked a little sheepish. "I don't know what made me say that. I guess I thought you were so excited over your foal that you might forget to keep your voice down."

"It's okay," I said, wondering why he didn't re-member that the more excited I get, the more quiet I get. But, then, this was a pretty exciting morning for him, too.

He reached for the coffeepot.

"I'll make breakfast," I said.

Breakfast is a pretty sketchy meal at our house except on weekends. Then it can get to be a kind of production. Usually Mom makes popovers or cinnamon rolls. I don't know which I like better.

It just so happened that I had never made a real breakfast in my life until this morning. I knew it wouldn't be a production or anywhere near one. But unlike some men, my dad is almost totally worthless in a kitchen. He says himself that he can hardly boil water without burning it. So I knew that whatever I did with the eggs and bacon, it would be better than anything he could do.

I fixed the coffee first, and when it started percolating, I got out the other stuff.

"How do you want your eggs?" I asked.

"Over easy," he replied, not looking up from last evening's *Monterey Herald*. He was sitting at the little table under the window where we eat breakfast during the week. On weekends we eat breakfast in the dining room. In style, sort of.

"He *would* want them over easy," I said to myself, doubting that I would be able to turn them without breaking the yolks.

Finally I had everything ready, and it didn't look too bad. I had managed to break one of the egg yolks, but the bacon was done just right and so was the toast. I put the plate down in front of him, and he folded the paper and put it aside.

"Looks good," he said. "Where's yours?"

"I'm not hungry."

"You'd better eat something. A glass of milk, fruit juice. Something."

I shook my head. "I'm just not hungry," I repeated.

It was the truth. I felt all churned up inside. The last hour had been too exciting for me. I couldn't have swallowed anything.

"You can have breakfast later with Mom," he said.

"I'll probably be hungry by then."

I watched him eating the breakfast I had fixed for him. He seemed to be enjoying it, though he wouldn't ever think to say so.

I really like my dad. For one thing, he's very dependable. If he isn't at the school bus stop, where I get off each afternoon, there's sure to be a very good reason for it. He gets off work around three when I get out of school, and it's mighty seldom I ever have to walk the long steep climb up to our house. I know he loves me, and sometimes he shows it. Like the time he drove me all the way to the Community Hospital when Missy was dying so I could leave my book there for her to read. She had liked it, too; she told me so. It was the very last time I saw her.

The only serious difference Dad and I have ever had was when he decided to buy me a horse and teach me equitation. I was afraid of horses. But I didn't put up a real fight about it because of Martin. He was my brother, five years older than I, who died of leukemia when I was five and he was ten. Martin was crazy about horses the way my dad is. I thought I had to make it up to Dad for his loss of Martin, and so I learned to ride. Missy helped me a lot during that time. I really miss her.

That all happened when I was ten. Now I'm twelve and I have learned to ride. There's still a lot I don't know, but I'm no longer afraid of horses. I love them just as Dad does. Especially Ethan and Merry Jo. And now Little Missy.

Dad got up from the table. "Thanks for the breakfast, Melinda. I think now I'll go out and check Merry Jo. The afterbirth may have come by this time."

He took up the lantern and left for the barn, and I put his dirty dishes in the sink and ran cold water on them. Then I followed him out.

He had picked up an old bucket in the tack stall and was going with it into Merry Jo's stall. I was right at his heels.

"It's here," he said, stooping to pick up a small mound of pinkish, grayish, slippery-looking stuff. He held it up and examined it, then put it in the bucket.

"Looks all right to me. Dr. Vance will check it out when he comes. I'm going to the house now to call him. It's a little early, but you might as well feed the horses."

By this time it was quite light outside. I slid the big

door open that leads into the paddock, then went into the tack stall for some hay. Enough light came in from outside so I didn't need the lantern for this. I was going to feed Ethan first. I could see him standing in the paddock looking toward the barn. As I emerged from it, he came trotting up to me, nickering pleasantly.

"Hi, Ethan," I greeted him.

He is the Morgan Dad bought for me two years ago when I first started to ride. He is a bright chestnut with a perfect disposition and a perfect way of going. Dad says he is the easiest riding horse he ever sat on. And he's beautiful!

He dropped his nose at once to the hay when I threw it down, and I patted him and told him all about Merry Jo's baby. I can't honestly say he appeared to be much interested as he munched his hay.

Now it was Merry Jo's turn.

She and her foal were standing quietly in a corner of the stall as I slid the door open and went in with the hay. Merry Jo nickered, and Little Missy stuck her head out at me. I touched her nose and felt the hairs matted there on it. Her eyes were big like her mother's and set wide apart. Now that she was dry, I could see she was a funny rust color, the color most foals are when they're born. Her tail was just a little furry nothing at the end of her body, but she switched it now and then. Her ears were small and pointed toward me as I set the lantern down and moved toward her. She didn't seem a bit afraid, and Merry Jo didn't seem to object. I smoothed the warm little body and put my arm around the straight-up little neck. Quickly she drew away from me. I was being too familiar on first acquaintance!

2

Little Missy

When I got back to the kitchen, Mom had come downstairs and was having coffee. In her bathrobe!

"How come you aren't dressed?" I said.

She set her mug down and came toward me. "Congratulations, Melinda! I hear you have a fine little filly."

She gave me a kiss and a hug.

"How come you're in your bathrobe?"

"I'm feeling lazy this morning. But as soon as I've finished my coffee, I'm going to get dressed. Then I want to see Little Missy."

I started toward the phone, which hangs on the wall near the kitchen sink, just as Dad came pounding downstairs.

I waited until he came into the kitchen.

"Okay if I ask Diana to come see Little Missy?"

Diana is my best friend. She lives down the road from me, and we are in the same class in Middle School.

Dad shook his head. "Not today, I think. Better let Merry Jo just see people she knows today. Diana can come tomorrow if she wants to."

So I called Diana and told her about Little Missy and that she could come see the foal tomorrow when we got back from church.

Diana didn't sound too thrilled about the foal, but she said she'd come by and see it sometime tomorrow. Diana isn't much interested in anything that doesn't concern her directly, but sometimes she surprises you. Like the time right after Missy died when she asked me to go to the movies with her and Dwight, her brother, the boy I've been in love with for two years. For a birthday present he had given her a visit to the movie of her choice with a friend of her choice and she had chosen me. And Dwight had taken us and *sat next to me*. It was the most exciting evening I have ever lived. To Dwight, who is seventeen, I'm just his kid sister's friend. Unfortunately.

Dad left the house before I hung up, and Mom was just leaving the kitchen when I put the receiver back.

"How about me getting some breakfast while you're dressing?" I asked her.

"I'd love it. Some bacon and toast. No eggs."

I decided to scramble a couple of eggs for myself; I was hungry by this time. We were certainly getting a late start on the day. Here it was after eight o'clock and Mom not even dressed yet and all the baking and marketing to do. Little Missy's arrival had sure thrown our family into a tailspin.

We were just finishing breakfast when in drove Dr. Vance in his pickup specially built to hold the medicine and tools a vet needs. Mom and I both got up from the little table by the window and went out to see what he would do about the mare and foal. It would be Mom's first look at Little Missy. I was feeling pretty important as I greeted Dr. Vance. Dad joined us, and we all went to the barn.

Merry Jo and the filly were both on their feet. At first I couldn't see Little Missy, but then suddenly I did. She was on the other side of her mother, peeking around at us, her delicate little head under Merry Jo's neck. Merry Jo nickered as I walked into the stall. She didn't seem at all excited to see the other three people. Of course she knew my father and mother, but she didn't know Dr. Vance all that well.

Little Missy started to come toward me, but as the vet came farther into the stall, Merry Jo moved so that the filly was out of sight on her other side.

"Let's put a halter on the mare," said Dr. Vance.

We have never made our horses wear halters when they are in their stalls. But I could see at once that it would be a good thing to put her halter on the mare now, with a lead shank attached to it. Horses aren't so dumb. They know that when you have them haltered you have pretty good control over them.

I got Merry Jo's halter out of the tack stall next door and slipped it on her. Then Dr. Vance gave her the tetanus shot. He refilled the syringe, took out a fresh needle, and was now ready for the foal. All we had to do was catch her!

Dad took hold of Merry Jo's lead shank, and Dr. Vance and I went after the filly. We moved slowly, trying to work her into a corner. Now Merry Jo began to show some concern. She kept nickering and trying to move around, but Dad held her and talked soothingly to her. At last I had my arms around the filly's chest and hind legs and, squatting down, held her against my chest. She struggled a little, but Dr. Vance worked quickly, and in a wink it was all over and Little Missy had had her first shot. Dad slipped off Merry Jo's halter, and she turned her head to nuzzle her foal, which had now rushed to her mother's side and was nursing.

"Never saw a prettier foal in all my life," said Dr. Vance.

"What do you think of her, Mom?" I asked.

She hadn't said a word about my new foal during all this time, and when I looked at her I was amazed to see her eyes swimming with tears.

"I'm such an old fool," she said. She sounded as if she really was mad at herself, but her voice was shaky. "It all seems so wonderful. And Merry Jo looked so proud when we opened her stall door. It just sort of got to me, I guess. She's a darling foal, Melinda. We'll have such fun watching her grow up."

"And Melinda will have the fun of training her," said Dad.

"Who told you how to hold a young foal?" Dr. Vance asked me. "You did it just right."

"I have a book on broodmares, and it tells you everything you need to know," I told him.

"Did it tell you that you want to hold foals like that several times a day when they are little?"

I shook my head.

"They haven't the strength yet to get away from you, and horses have long memories," he continued. "It's the only time in their lives that they aren't stronger than any human. But somehow they never forget that there was a time when they weren't. Besides, it makes a close contact between you and the foal and gives it confidence in you. The more you handle a foal, the better."

"Another good thing to do," said Dad, "is to pass a cloth over their backs every once in a while. They get to like the feel of it, and since this funny two-legged thing is doing something it likes, the foal begins to like and depend on the two-legged thing."

Mom laughed. "I can see you're really going to have your hands and your days full now, my daughter. Going to school, feeding Ethan and Merry Jo, training your filly, and helping me on Saturdays, you're going to be the busiest girl in Toro Estates."

"And the luckiest," added Dr. Vance. "Not many girls have a mare the quality of Merry Jo and a filly like this one. Take good care of her, young 'un—she's something really special."

Almost as if she were trying to show how very special she was, Little Missy hopped up into the air on her brand-new legs and almost fell over.

We all laughed.

"Nothing wrong with that one," said Dr. Vance as we all left the stall and I slid the heavy door shut. Merry Jo and her baby had had enough company for the time being.

The three grown-ups left the barn, and I went out to the paddock to talk to Ethan. I hadn't spent any time with him yet this morning, though I had fed him, and I thought I ought to make him realize that he was still my favorite. Ethan was a wild stallion when we first knew him. Dad bought him cheap and had him gelded, and then he trained him to be my saddle horse. That was before we even knew Missy, who willed me Merry Jo.

Ethan is the dearest horse you could even imagine. He has beautiful gaits, is a very dependable trail horse, and is very affectionate. He seems to know that he belongs to me. He also knows I always have a piece of carrot for him, too.

"Hi, Ethan!" I called to him as I came out of the barn.

He was at the far end of the paddock and came trotting up to me. I gave him the piece of carrot and rubbed his poll. That's the part of a horse's head that lies between the ears. Ethan loves to have me rub him there. He lowered his head to make it more convenient for me.

While I talked to him about Merry Jo's foal, I heard Dr. Vance start up his truck and drive away. Then Dad came to the paddock fence.

"Let's put Ethan in the ring and open the barn door so Merry Jo and Little Missy can come out into the sunshine."

"Okay," I said, and went into the barn for Ethan's halter.

He tried to follow me, and I had to slide the door almost shut. I haltered him and then led him over to the paddock gate, where Dad was waiting. I opened the gate and led Ethan out.

"You take him," I said. "I'll go back and open the stall door for Merry Jo."

"Come on, old fellow," Dad said to Ethan, and started him toward the ring.

I trotted back to the barn. I slid open the door that

leads from the barn into the paddock. Then I opened the door to Merry Jo's stall. The sun was well up now, and I told her how nice it was outside. Little Missy poked her head out of the stall and switched her tiny tail. She took a step out into the passage that runs between the stalls and the door into the paddock. From the stall Merry Jo nickered, and Little Missy stopped. She waited a moment, then took another step forward. Now she could see into the paddock. I wondered what she thought of the bright sunshine. I wondered if she would be afraid of her shadow the way Bucephalus, Alexander the Great's horse, had been afraid of his. That had been a story in our reader last year. I had really enjoyed that story, though I could remember a time when I couldn't have cared less about a story concerning a horse. All that had changed since Dad had bought Ethan and I had learned to love and to ride him.

I stood just outside Merry Jo's stall, as still as a statue, and watched my little filly. She took another short step, and now she could poke her head out of the barn. And now Merry Jo began to emerge from her stall.

All at once with a rush and a leap Little Missy was in the paddock and trying to keep from falling down. If she noticed her shadow at all, she was too busy trying to keep her feet to pay attention to it. Merry Jo was right behind her, nickering worriedly. I didn't blame her, because that foal's antics were wonderful to behold. She tried to kick at the sky and fell down on one flank. I had been laughing until my sides ached, but now I was scared. I needn't have been. She picked herself up in a jiffy and was off across the paddock, Merry Jo trotting heavily after her.

I heard Dad laughing over at the paddock gate. I walked over and joined him outside the paddock.

"Merry Jo's going to have her hands full with that one," he said. "Like an old hen with a duckling."

"I'm worried that she'll hurt herself trying to do acrobatics before she's firm on her legs," I said.

Dad shook his head, smiling. "Old Mother Nature will take care of all that," he told me. "If something frightened the filly, she might overreact and get hurt. But as long as she just plays as she wants to, it's good for her."

We stood silently watching the pair of them. Little Missy, noticing us all of a sudden, came down to the gate, Merry Jo following her. I put my hand between the fence boards, and the filly sniffed it. Then she turned away, walked a few paces, and lay down. Merry Jo immediately moved over to where she lay.

"I guess she's tired out with all the cavorting," Dad said. "We'd better go in now and find out what your mom wants us to bring home in the way of groceries."

I looked around at him in surprise. "Isn't she going with us?"

"Not this morning. She's not feeling very well."

"What's wrong with her?"

He shrugged. "Nothing serious. Just a little under the weather."

So that's why she had come down to breakfast in her bathrobe. Of course there was nothing unusual in somebody feeling under the weather, as Dad put it. Still, my mom is one of those people who is always on deck. She's the one who is always there to take care of Dad and me. Never has a cold, never has a headache. Never seems tired, though I suppose there are times when she must feel very tired. Of course, she's getting on in years. Thirty-seven now. I vowed as we walked toward the old house and mounted the stairs to the screened back porch that I would try to be more helpful from now on. I think I do my chores on Saturday with a pretty good will. But now I made up my mind that I would try to take on some of the things Mom has been doing that I could do almost as well now that I'm twelve. Like washing up the dishes at night all by myself. We don't have a dishwasher.

3

Mom Makes News

The next day Mom didn't go to church, either.

"God will forgive me in the circumstances," she said.

What was going on? I wondered. She hadn't gone shopping with Dad and me yesterday, and now here she was staying home from church. I began to feel frightened. What were they keeping from me? What were these circumstances she was referring to? Clearly, something was wrong with her. A lot of things could be wrong with her, now that she was thirty-seven. Hadn't my brother Martin died of leukemia at the age of ten? Were they trying to keep from me the fact that my mother had cancer? I was determined to find out, and soon.

So we had no sooner left our driveway and started down the valley road to church than I turned to Dad and asked, "What's the matter with Mom?"

"Nothing serious," he replied.

"That's not the answer I want. I'm getting very worried about her. I want to know."

He sighed and shifted his weight behind the wheel. "We probably shouldn't have kept it from you so long. We wanted to be perfectly sure. But now that we are sure, you might as well know."

While he spoke I could feel a tightness building up in my chest. Without realizing it, I was holding my breath.

"Your mom's two months' pregnant."

I let out my breath in a long sigh. So she wasn't sick, after all. She was just going to have a baby!

"I hope you're pleased," he said.

Was I? I honestly didn't know.

"Are you?" he insisted.

"I don't know yet," I replied truthfully. "It's the last thing I would have thought of. I was sure she had something very bad, like Martin. It's a relief to know it's nothing like that. I'm glad about that, anyway."

He seemed satisfied with this, and we rode the rest of the way in silence, both of us busy with our own thoughts. Of course, my mind was turning over this really astounding news. Was I glad? Offhand, I'd say I wasn't. What change would a new baby bring to our family? I'd be a built-in baby-sitter, for one thing, and I wasn't too pleased with that idea. I would have to share my parents' love with their new child. But since I would be thirteen years old when this baby was born, I didn't have to worry too much about having my nose put out of joint, as they say. By the time it could take my place as my father's riding companion or my mother's helper, I'd be through college. And it might be fun to have a live doll to play with. I had missed my dolls.

Suddenly a thought sprang at me, and my heart leaped up, as the poem says. This baby would take the place of Martin! Dad's son would be restored to him. Because this baby would be a boy. I felt it in my bones.

As we parked at the church and joined each other outside the car, I said to Dad, "I think I'm glad."

"Good girl," he replied, and gave my shoulders a strong squeeze.

During the homily, which was fairly boring, my thoughts wandered to the coming baby, and along with those thoughts came a disturbing one. Last year we had decided to turn Dad and Mom's big walk-in closet into a second bathroom. Their bedroom was plenty large enough to accommodate wardrobe closets. We really needed that second bathroom. But now there would have to be a crib in their bedroom. Besides that, it cost money to have babies. The doctor, the hospital, et cetera, et cetera. Would there be enough saved up by this time for a baby and a bathroom, too?

"I'm afraid not," my father answered when I put the question to him on our way home from church. "I think we'll just have to forget all about that second bathroom for a while."

I felt disappointed because, as Diana had once pointed out to me, we are the only family on our road with just one bathroom. When I'd reported this to my father, he had said, "We're the only family on this road with horses, too. That should give us as much prestige as having two toilets."

As I was remembering this, he spoke.

"I've decided to enclose a toilet on the back porch. That won't cost much, and we've needed it. We need it more now."

"How about Mom's job?" I asked.

"Her boss says she can stay as long as she wants to, and after the baby comes he will give her a leave of absence until she's able to come back to work."

When we got home, Mom was in the kitchen making brunch. I could see popover pans waiting on the counter.

"She knows," Dad announced before I could say anything.

Mom turned from the mixing bowl, a question in her eyes.

"It's okay with me," I said.

We threw our arms around each other, and Dad came and threw his arms around both of us. We all three were laughing.

Mom freed herself. "Can't you be just a little glad, Melinda?"

"I think I am glad," I said. "Not as glad as when we learned that Merry Jo was in foal, but still glad."

"Your enthusiasm overwhelms me," she replied, and turned on the electric mixer.

I went up to change into my playclothes (I still call them that), and then I phoned Diana to invite her to come see Little Missy. She told me they were all going out to brunch. All except Dwight. She invited me to go, too.

"My mother said it was okay to ask you," she added.

I thought a minute. If Dwight had been going, I would have said yes. Still, even without Dwight it would be fun to go to brunch. We aren't a family that eats out very often. Too expensive. And then, of course, we've been saving up for the new bathroom. I remembered that Mom likes us to spend Sunday together because we don't see much of one another during the week; we're all so busy. Still, I was pretty sure she'd let me accept Diana's invitation. Then, suddenly, I thought of Little Missy. I hadn't had more than a few minutes with her so far today, and now was the crucial time for holding her. I decided to have my brunch here at home.

"Thanks a lot, Diana," I told her, "but I think I'd rather stay home today and work with my foal. She's at a very important stage in her development right now."

"Okay," Diana said, sounding as if she didn't care one way or another. "See you after brunch."

We rang off, and I went out to the barn.

Little Missy came right over to me when I went into the paddock. I cradled her in my arms, and she struggled for a few seconds, then settled down and let me hold her. Her little body felt bony and warm. Merry Jo watched us but didn't make any objection to the way I was handling her baby.

I let the foal go, then went into the barn and got Ethan's saddle and bridle. I carried them out to the riding ring, where he was waiting for me. And I mean really waiting. He was right up at the gate with his head over it, and he nickered loudly when he saw me approaching. Poor old guy, his nose had been out of joint ever since yesterday with the arrival of the filly. Now it was his turn for some attention. I put the saddle on the rail of the ring and laid the bridle across it. Then I went back to the barn for my curry comb, brush, and hoof pick.

Though it was still not quite February, spring comes early to the Carmel Valley, and I noticed as I rubbed the curry comb over Ethan's back and flanks that he was already beginning to shed some winter hair. He has a very heavy winter coat, and he looked now as woolly as a bear. I would be glad when he had his short coat again and was sleek and shiny. I groomed him well, then put the saddle and bridle on him. He seemed glad of all the attention, and even reached around to nose my bottom when I was cleaning his front feet.

I worked him for half an hour, going on both leads and both diagonals. And he went well for me. Deciding it was about time for brunch to be ready, I rode him to the middle of the ring and dismounted. I removed the saddle and bridle and brushed him down again, rubbing him hard with an old towel where the girth had encircled him. I carried the tack to the barn and then started for the house. And was I ever hungry!

Mom was putting the finishing touches on breakfast as I crossed to the kitchen sink to wash my hands. The popovers had popped way up. Mom had opened the oven door and put some plates in to warm.

"Take up the popovers, Melinda. I put a plate in the oven for them."

Mom was already putting the rest of our brunch on the other warm plates. I carried the popovers into the dining room and was surprised to see a rather large package at my place, all wrapped in fancy paper and ribbon. I couldn't imagine why it should be there, since my birthday wasn't until August and today was no special occasion.

I helped carry in the plates, and then we all sat down.

"What's this all about?" I asked, looking down at the package.

"Open it up and see," said Mom.

"You're going to look great in it," Dad said.

I drew the envelope out from under the ribbon with a pleasant feeling of excitement. It is always fun to have something new to wear, and it doesn't happen to me so often that I'm not thrilled when it does.

The card had a picture of a mare and a foal on it, and inside a note said, "To a fine young horsewoman, with love from Mom and Dad."

So whatever it was, it had something to do with horses.

Dad and Mom were letting their breakfast get cold as they watched me. I finally got the ribbon and paper off and lifted up the lid of the box.

I couldn't have guessed in a million years what lay inside. It was a little leather halter! So Dad had been joking. I took it out and held it up. It was like a toy. In every way it was like a full-size halter, only it was tiny.

"For Little Missy," I said. "Thank you, thank you ever so much."

"Now eat your breakfast before it gets stone-cold," said Mom.

But I had to finger the little halter some more.

"When can we put it on her?" I asked.

"We'll try it on her this morning and let her wear it for a few minutes tomorrow. Then we'll put it on her for a little while every day," Dad told me.

I could hardly wait for breakfast to be over, I was so eager to see the filly in her new halter. But first there were the dishes to do. I started rinsing out the sink and turning hot water into it, but Mom shoved me to one side.

"I'll take care of this," she said. "You run along and try on the halter."

I hesitated, remembering all my good intentions of such a short time before. But I did so want to try the halter on the foal. Mom understood that, the way she understands so much of what I am feeling.

"Sure you don't mind?" I said.

"Very sure."

So I took her at her word, called to Dad, and together we went to the barn.

I held Little Missy while Dad fitted the halter on her. She didn't like this one bit, and neither did Merry Jo. The mare began to be really belligerent, so I went in and got her halter and put it on her. It worked like magic, and she settled down and let Dad finish haltering the foal. When he turned her loose, the filly went sort of staggering off, shaking her head, Merry Jo tagging after her and trying to comfort her.

Finally Little Missy stopped shaking her head, and then Dad said it was time to take the halter off. I walked over to her, and she decided to play games. She kicked up her heels at me and went dashing off.

Dad laughed. "The longer she wears it, the better."

But Little Missy's moods were subject to change without notice. Even as he spoke, she wheeled and came charging toward me. Just as she was about to knock me down, I reached out and grabbed her. By the halter. I quickly unstrapped it and slid it past her nose.

"In a day or so we'll start training her to lead," said Dad. "Then we can take her out on the trail with her mother."

"Really?" I said, surprised. "We won't have to wait until she is weaned to take Merry Jo out?"

He shook his head. "We can have them both on the trail in a couple of weeks. Just as soon as the filly has a little more strength in her legs. It will be good for them both."

This put a whole new look on the new year. In spite of a new foal Merry Jo would be able to take Dad out on the trail when the first real spring days arrived. I was glad, because while I'm allowed to ride alone now that I am twelve, I always enjoy it more when Dad is along with me.

Early in the afternoon Diana came to see Little Missy. Diana had changed out of her brunch clothes and was wearing jeans and a T-shirt that said "Carmel-by-the-Sea" on it. I was dressed the same way, only my T-shirt said "I ♡ New York." My grandmother had sent it to me; she lives there.

Diana was very nice about the filly.

"She's real cute, Melinda. Can I pet her?"

Little Missy had come up to the paddock fence and was sticking her hairy little nose up between the boards.

"Go ahead," I said.

Diana put her hand between the boards and was trying to rub Little Missy's ears. But before she could get really started Merry Jo sauntered over and got between the fence and her foal. She was very nice about it, but it was plain she didn't want Diana to lay a hand on her baby. The foal poked her head around under her mother's neck. Then she gave a sudden kick and went tearing off across the paddock. Merry Jo turned to follow her more slowly.

"When will you have to sell her?" asked Diana.

If she had hit me in the face, she couldn't have astonished me more than her question did. Sell Little Missy! The idea hadn't occurred to me, and I could find no room for it in my wildest imagining now.

"What do you mean, sell her?" I demanded.

"Just what I say," returned Diana, as if she had asked the most ordinary question anybody ever heard. "You surely can't keep three horses."

"Why not?"

"Isn't it pretty expensive, keeping a horse?"

"Not when you take care of it yourself. Hay isn't all that much, and Dad and I do all the work of caring for them. It's when you have to board a horse that it really costs a lot."

"How soon before you can start riding her?"

"We can start training her in a couple of years and ride her hard when she's three."

"How much could you get for her if you sold her?" Diana asked.

"I don't know, and I don't even want to think about it. Little Missy is not for sale, now or at any time in the future."

I meant every word of it.

Diana turned away from the paddock, her interest in the filly at an end. "So what else is new?"

Diana is apt to say things like that. It leaves you with the feeling that nothing very interesting happens around your house, but at the same time, I knew that nothing as interesting as the birth of Little Missy had happened at *her* house recently. Even if she did go to brunch nearly every Sunday and saw a lot more movies than I did. Diana's dad is a lawyer and rich.

"Want to go in and play a game of backgammon?" I asked.

"Sure," said Diana, and we started toward the house.

I had decided to tell her about the new baby, but I thought I'd wait until we were alone in my room.

4

Diana's Great Idea

When we went inside, Dad was watching TV and Mom was reading the Sunday paper. She looked up to greet Diana.

"How's everything at your house, Diana?"

"Just fine, thank you," Diana said politely.

"Same here," said Mom, returning to her paper.

I got out the backgammon board and put it on the card table that serves as a desk for me. Diana has a real desk, and I am hoping to have one someday, but, of course, the bathroom comes first.

"Before we start, I have some news for you, Diana."

"What?"

"Guess."

She thought for a moment. "I know. You're going to start on the new bathroom."

I had told her about our plans some time ago, and she had agreed it was the thing to do. That was when she informed me that we were the only family on the road with just one.

"You'll never guess, so I might as well tell you. My mom is going to have a baby."

"You're kidding!"

"No, I'm not. And in case you're wondering, I'm actually glad."

"I wouldn't be," Diana said firmly.

"You might be if you had lost Dwight when he was ten, as I lost my brother. I know this baby will be a boy, and for my dad and mom it will be almost like having Martin back again."

We sat for a few moments in silence, the backgammon game forgotten.

"There's just one drawback," I said. "We won't be able to afford a new bathroom and a new baby, too. Dad said so today. Instead, he's going to enclose a toilet on the back porch."

"That's a good idea," said Diana. "You actually need a downstairs toilet more than you need a second bathroom." For a moment she studied me as if she were trying to make up her mind whether or not to say what she wanted to say. At last she spoke. "What you really need, though, or will before long, is a family room."

"Are you crazy?" I demanded. "How could we ever afford to build a family room? It would take years to save up that kind of money."

She was right, of course. We did need a family room. I had no place to entertain my friends except the living room, which is one reason I don't have any friends except Diana. It's not much fun for kids to visit if your parents are there all the time. They feel shy, and nothing feels the same as it does when we are just kids, alone, like at Diana's or on the school grounds. But I knew a family room for the Ross family was *out*. Definitely.

While I had been thinking this, I had let my eyes wander out to where, across the barnyard, I could see Little Missy and Merry Jo moving around their paddock. Ethan was standing quietly near the gate to the riding ring. My spirits perked up as I watched them. Not many girls had as much as I did, even if I didn't have a family room.

"Hey," said Diana suddenly, and I withdrew my gaze from the horses. "I've got a neat idea. You could turn your back porch into a family room. That wouldn't cost so much. The floor and ceiling are already there, and three walls."

I nodded, my mind in a daze. What a terrific idea! Was it possible? I dumped the dice I had been holding and got to my feet.

"Come on," I said. "Let's go down and take a look at the porch."

Together we raced down the stairs, making such a racket on the bare boards that Mom called out, "Where's the fire?"

We didn't bother to answer as we raced through the kitchen, and through the door leading into the screened back porch. It was a good-size porch, plenty big enough to accommodate a small powder room, and continuing to enclose that end of the porch, there could be a very decent wardrobe closet. Besides being a family room for us kids, with a bed-sofa in it, it could be a guest room now that the baby would need the third upstairs bedroom. I began to feel excitement growing in me. Even without the third bedroom, I could still have a friend stay over.

"Let's go tell my folks," I said.

Off we rushed to the living room.

"Diana's got a marvelous idea," I burst out, interrupting the TV program, and causing Mom to put aside her paper.

"Out with it," said Dad, touching the blab-off.

"She says why don't we turn the screened back porch into a family room?"

Total silence followed my announcement. Mom stared at Diana as if she were seeing something strange and wonderful. Dad was staring at Mom, and I could almost see his mind working. A slow smile was spreading across his face.

"Out of the mouths of babes," exclaimed Mom. She looked over at Dad. "Cal, where have our brains been all this time? Yammering about a second bathroom when all the time what we really need is a family room. Especially now with a baby coming. We'd have a place to keep it when it starts crawling around." She rose from the sofa. "Let's go take a look."

We all trooped out to the back porch.

"It's perfectly feasible," declared Dad. Echoing what I had had in mind, he continued, "We could close off the far end of the room where your washer-dryer is now with a cupboard for them, a clothes closet, and a small powder room. And it wouldn't cost much. Not over four thousand dollars at the most."

I hadn't felt so excited since the arrival of Little Missy. We would have a family room and a downstairs toilet to boot. Perfect!

"How long would it take to build it, Dad?"

"Hardly more than three or four months, working in my spare time."

"Then it could be ready before the baby comes."

He shook his head slowly. "Not this year, honey. Remember I told you there wouldn't be enough money for a baby and a bathroom, too. The same holds good for a family room." He reached out and pulled me toward him, seeing the disappointment in my face. But I twisted away from him. I really did. I don't know when I've felt so let down, and I knew that if anyone spoke a word of sympathy to me, I would start to bawl.

"How about that game of backgammon?" Diana asked.

I looked at her gratefully and nodded. Though she thinks mostly about herself, there are times when Diana can surprise you. Like now.

We two went upstairs, leaving my mom and dad walking around and around the back porch, speculating on how well it would convert to a family room and marveling that they hadn't thought of it themselves.

"Good for Diana," I heard Mom say. "Sometimes that child just amazes me."

We had hardly started our game when Diana said, "I have news for you, too."

I looked across the board at her, waiting, the dice in my hand.

"I'm going to get my ears pierced next Thursday after school."

"You are!"

She nodded. "Why don't you get yours done?"

"I don't think my mother would let me."

"You won't know till you ask her."

"Does it cost much?"

Diana shrugged. "I don't know. Our doctor is going to do it."

Then it was out for me. We didn't have doctors unless it was absolutely necessary. Getting my ears pierced wasn't absolutely necessary. Though I really would have liked having it done. It would make me feel more grown up. And then you would have to have some earrings to wear. It would be fun to have earrings.

We finished the game, which I won, and then Diana decided she had to go home. On our way downstairs she whispered to me, "Do you want me to ask her?"

"About my ears?" I asked.

She nodded.

"Okay, if you want to," I said.

So as we reached the lower hall, Diana stuck her head into the living room.

"Mrs. Ross, I'm going to get my ears pierced next Thursday after school. Would it be okay if Melinda went with me and had hers done, too?"

Mom spoke immediately without a moment's thought. "I hardly think so, Diana. We like Melinda just the way she is."

"I'd really like to do it, Mom," I said with pleading in my voice.

"Maybe later on, dear. You're still a little girl. I'd like you to stay that way just a little longer. You'll be grown up for such a long time."

I didn't say anything, but I felt sulky, and I tried to look as sulky as I could, which is about as sulky as anybody can look.

"Well, g'bye all," Diana said, and we all said good-bye, and I let her out the front door. She gave me a sympathizing look before she started down the stairs off the front porch. I wasn't sure whether it was because I couldn't get my ears pierced or because she knew my mom was pregnant. If the latter, then the joke was on her, because the more I thought about it the more I thought I didn't mind a bit that Mom was pregnant.

I returned to my room to finish the theme we always have to hand in on Monday morning. Our English teacher, Mrs. Holt, is real old-fashioned. She thinks the only way to learn to write properly is to write. So we have to hand in a theme every Monday morning. She corrects it for organization, development, spelling, and punctuation and hands it back so we can see the mistakes we made. Sometimes she gives us a subject, and sometimes we can choose our own. But no matter what, we have to hand in a theme every Monday. Most of the kids hate doing the themes and hate Mrs. Holt, but I am not one of them. Two years ago my friend Missy encouraged me to write, and so I did, and I liked doing it so much that I have decided to be a writer when I grow up.

My theme for tomorrow was the birth of Little Missy. I wrote it just about the way I have described it here, only I went more into Merry Jo's background and how I happened to be her owner. I titled my theme "Little Missy."

5

Little Missy Entertains

Dad was already waiting next day after school when the bus stopped to let the Toro Estates kids off. As Diana and I got into the car, he lifted up a rope coiled on the front seat.

"This is Little Missy's rump rope," he informed me.

He handed it to me to hold. It was a rope with about the same thickness as a clothesline.

"Rump rope?" I asked.

He nodded. "We call it that because I'll make a wide loop of it and put it right around her body. At the same time I'll have a lead rope attached to her halter. Then I'll pull on the halter rope, and she won't move.

So then I'll pull on the rump rope, and when she feels it tighten against her rump she'll come forward. When she moves forward, I'll let up on the rump rope and gently pull on the lead rope. In no time she'll learn to lead. And when she is leading well and dependably, we can take her out of the paddock with her mother, lead her around the yard, and eventually take her out on the trail, ponying her."

"What do you mean by 'ponying'?" I asked.

"When you lead a horse while riding another, the horse you are leading is being 'ponied,' " he told me.

We let Diana off at her house, and during the rest of the long climb from the valley road up to our house, I thought about the two new horse terms I had learned: "rump rope" and "pony." Of course I knew what a pony was, but I had never before heard the word used for a horse being led.

The minute I get home from school, I have to run upstairs and change my clothes. Now that I go to Middle School, my mother won't let me wear jeans. She says clothes have a lot to do with mood, and now that I have moved into the higher grades, I must take school more seriously than I did before, when I was just a little kid. Wearing dresses instead of jeans doesn't hamper me because we wear uniforms for all our field games at Middle School. In a way, wearing different clothes for school makes me feel a little more grown up, like dressing to go to a job. And I have to admit that it does make me feel a little more serious about school than I did before. But that may be because now I'm almost a teenager.

When I came out to the barnyard after changing, Dad was already in the paddock next to the barn, putting her halter on Little Missy.

"Halter Merry Jo and keep her out of the way while I start working with the filly," he told me.

But first I had to go to the ring, where Ethan was already reaching his head over the gate toward me, knowing that he would have a carrot when I got home from school.

"Hi, Ethan!" I called to him, and he nickered back at me like the gentleman he is.

He took the carrot gently, and I rubbed his poll while he chewed it. Then I ran to the barn to get Merry Jo's halter.

As I slipped it on her, Dad said, "She's not going to like my forcing her foal to do something she isn't going to want to do, so you'll have to keep a good hold on her."

"I will," I promised.

Dad had made a slipknot in the new rope, and now he shook out a loop that looked to be about the length of Little Missy's small body. He gently lowered it over her. She didn't like this much and started to back away from him. Then he pulled up slightly on the rope, and when she felt it tighten around her hind legs, she stopped backing. Now he took a short hold of the lead rope attached to her halter, all the time holding onto the rump rope.

Meanwhile Merry Jo was nickering and moving around, and I had to give some attention to her. I had placed her in a corner of the paddock as far away from the foal and Dad as I could. It was plain she wanted to get to where they were.

Now I saw Dad gently pull on the lead rope, and Little Missy hung back. So, still holding the lead rope in its same position, he pulled up on the rump rope. Instantly she moved forward, and he backed a step away from her, still applying the rump rope. Step after step she came after him. Little Missy was being led for the very first time!

When she stopped, Dad went to her and rubbed her back and told her what a fine little filly she was, and she tried to switch her tail, which was tucked behind the rump rope.

"Now let's try it again," he said.

The whole routine was repeated exactly like the first time. Little Missy refused to respond to the lead rope and had to feel the rump rope. Time after time this happened, while I talked soothingly to Merry Jo and tried to reassure her as to her baby's safety. She had relaxed a lot.

Finally Dad twitched off the rump rope and un-snapped the lead rope from the foal's little halter.

"That's enough for the first time," he said. "We'll work with her again tomorrow, and tomorrow you can try to lead her."

I slipped off Merry Jo's halter, and she went quickly to meet her foal, who was already running to meet her mother. They met in the middle of the paddock, and immediately Little Missy stuck her small nose under her mother's belly and started nursing. She needed comfort after all that terrible manhandling!

"There's one thing you must know and remember, Melinda, before you try to lead the filly. Don't ever pull on her neck. Sure, you have the strength, now that she's so little, to pull her along on all four feet, but don't ever do it. The bones in a foal's neck are delicate and soft, and you can cause an injury they'll never recover from. That's why we use a rump rope. You can't hurt them by pulling on a rump rope, but you sure can on a halter rope."

"I'll remember," I replied.

On Friday when Mrs. Holt handed back our themes, I discovered I had gotten an A. Right after she had handed them back and we were looking them over to see what we had done wrong, she asked for our attention.

"I learned something interesting this week when I read your papers," she began. "I was surprised to discover that a member of this class is a breeder of Morgan horses. Does anyone know who this is?"

Of course, Diana raised her hand. "It's Melinda Ross."

I was sure surprised to be singled out for this kind of attention, and I could feel my face getting red.

"Melinda, would you like to take a few minutes to tell us something about Morgans and your little filly in particular?"

I rose and took a moment to gather my thoughts.

"To begin with," I said, "I wouldn't call myself a breeder. Not yet, anyway. I inherited a champion Morgan mare in foal to a champion stallion. This foal is a really beautiful little filly, and she's going to make a super mare."

"Why do you call your horse a Morgan?" someone asked, and I told about the music teacher in New England at the beginning of the nineteenth century, named Justin Morgan, who had this small stallion which could do just about anything and which established the Morgan breed. There were other questions, and most of them I could answer. Then someone said, "Can we come and see your foal?"

I wasn't prepared for this, and for a minute I didn't know what to say. I felt I should check it out with Dad or Mom before saying yes, but neither of them was home, and I wasn't supposed to phone Mom at the office unless it was a real emergency. Still, I didn't see what harm there could be if some of the class wanted to come and see Little Missy. She would be a whole week old and pretty used to people. Besides, I wanted awfully to show her off.

So I said it would be okay if they wanted to come

tomorrow, Saturday, and I gave them directions to my house.

"I'd like to see Little Missy, too, Melinda," said Mrs. Holt. "I have never seen a very young foal in all my life."

I said I would be glad to have her come, too, and then I sat down feeling kind of proud and important. Like I did when Dr. Vance came to check out Merry Jo and the foal.

"What time would you like us to be at your house, Melinda?" Mrs. Holt asked. "I think it would be better if we had a special time instead of drifting in off and on all day. I imagine your parents have things to do on Saturday like everybody else. What would be the best time, do you think?"

I considered for a moment. "How about ten-thirty?"

"Ten-thirty it is," declared Mrs. Holt. "By the way, how many would like to see Melinda's filly?"

About ten hands went up. Some others said they would come if they could get one of their parents to bring them.

When I met Dad at the bus stop at the end of the school day, he seemed pleased that I would be showing off the filly next day.

"We must groom Merry Jo and the filly within an inch of their lives. Ethan, too. And we'll show the barn. I bet most of these kids have never been inside a barn."

Mom was pleased, too, and even spent part of that evening making a big batch of cookies. There was already plenty of fruit juice on hand. It was going to be quite a party! My first since coming to the valley.

But long before then, and while I was trying to lead Little Missy around the paddock, Dad came out of the barn and stood watching us. Once in a while the filly would want to balk, and then I would pull up on the rump rope and she would start up again.

"I'd say she was doing very well for a one-week-old," Dad said as I led her over to him. "She's a smart little filly."

He rubbed her back and picked up each one of her feet. She didn't care much for this, but he persisted in his kindly way and finally persuaded her to trust him to lift her feet well off the ground.

"You know, I've been thinking," he said, straightening up and dusting his hands off. "Why don't we stage a one-girl gymkhana here tomorrow?"

"What do you mean?" I asked, slipping off Little Missy's halter. She whirled and went tearing across the paddock to her mother, then turned and looked back at me as if to say, "So there!" Dad and I laughed.

"What do I mean?" he repeated. "I mean that you would ride Ethan in the ring and put him through some paces. I think your friends ought to know what a good rider you are."

"What makes you think they'd be interested in

watching me ride? It might bore them to death."

"Nearly everybody likes to watch a good rider on horseback. Nearly everybody likes to watch a good horse. Haven't you ever noticed how people's interest in a TV ad perks up when it has a horse in it?"

I laughed. "Mine sure does."

"I've never been able to understand why they don't use horses more in ads," he went on. "Of course I could be prejudiced," he added, grinning, "but horses are mighty good attention getters. You wouldn't be taking any risks about boring your visitors if you rode Ethan for them tomorrow. Who knows? It might make some converts for the Morgan breed."

"Okay, Dad, if you're so set on it. Of course it means I'll have to clean my tack. Fortunately I have a clean saddle pad."

I have two saddle pads, a white one and a blue one, and I always make sure that one of them is clean.

So while Mom made cookies in the kitchen that evening, I sat on the floor of the back porch, under the single light globe, with my saddle and bridle, surrounded by various kinds of saddle soaps and oils and rags for polishing leather.

Some people hate to clean tack, but I sort of like to. The bridle is the hardest part because you have to take it all apart, and some of the straps are hard to get unbuckled. Usually you have to take a screwdriver and just pry the leather open. But when it is all clean and softened up again and back together with the bit polished and bright, you have a wonderful sense of accomplishment. Not a bit like housework. Or so I think.

I carried the saddle into the kitchen and set it over the back of one of the kitchen chairs and hung the bridle on the knob of the door into the dining room.

"My, that leather smells good!" Mom said, sniffing.

"So do the cookies," I said. "Mind if I snitch a couple?"

"Help yourself."

Next morning I woke up about seven-thirty and dressed quickly. Mom and Dad were still asleep. Fancy and I went quietly down the stairs and out to the barn.

It was February now, and though the sun hadn't quite cleared the eastern hills, the light was strong, and I could see it was going to be a fine day. Though the morning was chilly, spring was in the air. The hills were green in the growing light, and between the back porch and the barn our old plum tree was in full pink bloom.

I started to feed the horses. When I carried his alfalfa out to Ethan, I also took along the curry comb and brush. The hoof pick I slid into a pocket of my jeans. Shedding as he was, I knew it would take a long time to groom him properly. Merry Jo's coat was not as heavy as his. As for Little Missy, a few strokes of the brush along her back would take care of her.

By the time I had finished with Ethan, the sun was

over the ridge. My gelding looked a lot better and the ground around him was covered with chestnut-colored hair. Of course he might roll between now and when I saddled him, but a light brushing would take care of that. I decided to let Merry Jo eat in peace.

I started for the house and breakfast. I could see a light on in the kitchen, so I knew somebody was up.

"Good morning, daughter," Mom greeted me as I came into the kitchen. "Big day coming up. What's the weather like?"

"Chilly and sunny," I replied as I crossed to the sink to wash my hands.

Dad came sauntering into the kitchen, yawning mightily.

"I've fed the horses and groomed Ethan," I told him.

He nodded approval. "Too bad he isn't in his summer coat. But you two are going to look good no matter what."

I could only hope he was right.

Promptly at ten-thirty our visitors began to arrive. Mrs. Holt was among the first. I had saddled and bridled Ethan and had him tied to the ring fence. Head up, ears pricked, he was watching the cars as they drove in.

The minute Mrs. Holt caught sight of me, she exclaimed, "Melinda! You look smashing!"

I was wearing my jodhpurs, and even if I say so myself, I look good in my riding habit.

We stood around while I introduced everyone to Mom and Dad. Then, with Dad and me leading the way and Mrs. Holt, Mom, and the other parents bringing up the rear, we trooped across the barnyard to the paddock.

Little Missy was right at the paddock gate, eyes and ears alert. During this first week of her life, she had learned to enjoy attention. It was plain from the beginning that she was going to be a "people's horse." Now, to her evident delight, a whole group of people was approaching, and she was ready and willing to accept their admiration. As they lined up along the fence, she couldn't decide which one to greet first. She trotted back and forth, presenting her nose to be rubbed, then jerking it away to nuzzle someone else. Everyone wanted to pet her, and a dozen hands were reaching into the paddock while oh's and ah's and squeals of delight must have sounded pleasantly in her hairy little ears. All the while, her tail was switching joyously.

I had already haltered Merry Jo and hung her lead shank over the paddock fence. Now I took it up and went in to where she stood watching, a little removed from the gate, and snapped it to her halter.

"You may come into the paddock two at a time to pet Little Missy," Dad announced, and after a moment's polite hesitation, two of my classmates entered the paddock.

Little Missy welcomed them cordially and allowed

them to smooth her back. But when they tried to put an arm around her neck, she drew away. Merry Jo nickered once or twice, but I kept talking to her, and she stood quietly. I think she realized that as long as Dad and I were there, everything would be all right.

Two by two, the visitors came in to pet Little Missy. But by the time the fourth couple had entered, she decided she had had enough. Whirling, she tore off, bucking and kicking at the sky. It was quite a show, and it amused everyone.

I slipped off Merry Jo's halter, and she went trotting toward her foal. Little Missy ran to meet her mother and begin nursing. Most of the kids had never seen a foal nurse before, and they marveled at the difficult position a foal is forced to take, turning its head upside down to reach the nipples.

This put an end to the Little Missy show, and now it was my turn.

It had been a very long time since I had felt nervous at the idea of riding Ethan. But as I approached the ring this morning, with ten of my classmates following me, along with their parents and Mrs. Holt, to say nothing of my mom and dad, who, I knew, would want me to do well, I felt really nervous.

As I opened the gate and went into the ring, I heard Dad explaining to the group that I rode a jump-seat saddle, that my bridle was a single-rein snaffle with noseband or cavesson, and the bit a snaffle. I untied

Ethan, gathered up my reins, took hold of a handful of mane in my left hand, grabbed the cantle, or back of the saddle, with my right hand, and with my left foot in the left stirrup, lifted myself into the saddle. I slipped my right foot into the right stirrup, spoke to Ethan, and he moved into a brisk walk. I hadn't walked him long before I signaled a trot, and he went off smoothly, with me posting on the proper diagonal. This simply means that the rider rises as the horse's outside shoulder moves forward. You settle back in the saddle as the shoulder comes back.

I trotted around the ring a couple of times on each diagonal, and then I slowed Ethan to a walk and signaled a canter. Off he went on the correct lead. Since I was riding on the right-hand side of the ring, this means that Ethan reached forward with his left forefoot. I knew I was riding well because it all felt comfortable. As we cantered past the gate, Dad held up a hand, his thumb and forefinger making a nice O. Again, I stopped Ethan, reversed him, and signaled a canter on the other lead. Then it happened.

Just as we were coming past the gate for the second time, one of the boys in the group, Dick Masters, hoisted himself to the top of the fence. At the appearance of a sudden object above his head, Ethan shied violently, jumping sideways about fifteen feet. He had never shied with me before. Once on the trail, when a deer had popped out of the brush right in front of him, he had been startled enough to whirl, and I had managed to stay with him. But this was the first time he had ever shied.

It all happened in a matter of seconds. There wasn't really time to get scared. By some miracle I managed not to get thrown in the sudden force of the sideways motion. I did lose my right stirrup, but I got my foot back into it immediately. Though he was now standing still, I could feel how tense Ethan was. I could hear Dad ordering Dick off the fence and warning him never to make quick moves around horses. I called out that I was okay, then I walked Ethan over to the gate. Poor Dick was explaining that he hadn't known he was doing anything wrong and that he was sorry he had frightened my horse.

One of the girls said, "You sure are a neat rider, Melinda. I don't see why you didn't fall off."

"Because she *is* a neat rider," Dad assured her. "Now, Melinda, you must put Ethan into a canter again and come past the gate just as you did now. And this time everything will go all right. We have to get this scare out of his head."

So I put Ethan into a canter again. As we approached the gate this time around, I got ready for whatever might happen, tightening my reins a little and touching Ethan with my heel to let him know I was ready. But everything went off well. We circled one more time, then I rode him to the middle of the ring and dismounted.

Then it dawned on me! For the first time in my life I had ridden before an audience! It's true it wasn't much of an audience, but wanting to perform well for my classmates gave me an inkling of what it would be like when I rode in competition, as I would be doing next year.

I untacked Ethan and turned him loose in the ring. Everyone was most satisfactorily impressed with us both. I received many compliments on my riding and had the feeling I had gone up a notch in my classmates' estimate of me. It was a nice feeling.

Mom invited everyone into the house for fruit juice and cookies. We went in by the back porch as usual. There was a little horseplay among the boys as we mounted the steps, and everyone was talking. But by the time we reached the dining room, where Mom had everything ready, the kids were pretty much subdued. Mostly it was the parents who were talking now, and I thought that if only I had a family room, we kids would be in it making our own special conversation and leaving the parents to the dining room. Well, some-day. Meanwhile it was a real satisfaction to have my classmates here, eating Mom's cookies and drinking juice.

"Where's Diana?" Mrs. Holt asked suddenly. "Aren't you two special friends, Melinda?"

I nodded. "I guess her mother needed her this morn-ing. Besides, she's already seen Little Missy."

To tell the truth, I had wondered about Diana's

failing to show up. I know she has no interest in horses. And I know she likes to be the biggest toad in the puddle. This morning I was. Probably it was mean of me to think this way, especially since it was Diana who had thought of the family room. And maybe her mother *had* actually needed her. As you can see, I have my faults. Same as Diana.

"A nice bunch of kids," Dad said when we had waved the last car out of the yard.

"And a nice bunch of parents, too," echoed Mom. "I really like Mrs. Holt. We must have another party before too long."

"A cookout, maybe, when the weather warms up," I said. "I don't want an inside party until we get the family room."

"It'll be quite a while before you have an inside party then," Dad said.

6

In Training

By the following Monday I was leading Little Missy around and around the paddock, using the rump rope when she pulled back. But it wasn't often I had to use it. Little Missy learned fast!

The filly was getting prettier all the time. Her ribs didn't stick out so much, and between her big dark eyes a slight swelling had appeared. This gave her the "dish" face so much valued in Morgans.

On the day she was a month old, I was able to lead her *away from her mother*, and she came willingly. By this time she would allow me, without any sign of struggle, to pick up every one of her four feet in turn.

She was growing fast and beginning really to eat her mother's alfalfa hay instead of just sniffing at it. But she was still nursing regularly.

It was about this time that she started losing her baby coat. Dark patches began showing up on her muzzle and around her eyes. Then her chest began to show dark. She was going to be a liver chestnut like her sire and dam. Right now she looked moth-eaten.

She continued to be playful and friendly, though she liked to kick up her heels and buck. She'd had teeth since she was two weeks old, but she still didn't know what to do with a carrot.

On the day she was six weeks old, I began training her for showing her in hand. This means on a halter and lead rope. I had long ago decided I would show her in the next Golden West Championship Morgan Horse Show when it came to Monterey. This year it would start on June thirtieth and end on July second. Little Missy would be almost six months old then. I knew there were two classes I could enter her in: filly foals of 1978 and broodmare with 1978 foal. She was much too young for me to start training her seriously for showing, but there were things I could teach her, like running on the lead beside me and how to stand with her front feet perfectly in line, her back feet extended a little and her head held high.

Already our good friend Joe Fuller had come to trim her feet. He is the man who fits shoes on Ethan and

Merry Jo. He is a wizard when it comes to horse-shoeing, and he handled the filly so gently and patiently that he didn't scare her a bit.

It was really fun working with her. She loved the running part of it, and usually I had all I could do to hold her once she got started. It took several weeks before she learned not to go faster than I wanted to and not to kick and buck out of sheer joy. But part of the fun in training a foal is developing patience in yourself and then seeing a tiny bit of improvement as the weeks go by.

But I am getting ahead of my story.

The most exciting thing to happen during this period of her early training was taking her out on the trail for the first time. I confess I felt jumpy; she was still so little. But Dad reassured me. We had already been leading her around the paddock, Dad on Merry Jo and I on Ethan. And then around and around the barnyard. She had gone quietly and confidently. But this particular afternoon would be a real adventure for her.

"Even if she managed to break away from me," Dad said, "the filly would never run away from her mother. If something frightened her, like a deer or a rabbit, she might shoot off a little way, but she'd come right back again. Actually, we don't need to pony her. She could be loose right now to follow along with us. But I want her to get used to being ponied."

Usually when I go out on the trail, Fancy goes with

me. But today we shut her in the house. We didn't want her to do something silly and frighten the foal. If something should happen this first time out to frighten Little Missy badly, she might always and forever be a little trail shy. As Dr. Vance said, horses have long memories.

When we first started out, Little Missy didn't seem to know just what was expected of her. She had never been outside our barnyard before, and she hung back timidly. Dad gave a very gentle jerk on her lead rope and moved Merry Jo forward. Right away, the foal stated toward her mother. We were on the trail.

At first the trail is open meadow, then it climbs quite steeply, and suddenly you are in a pine forest, the ground underfoot carpeted with pine needles.

I was riding ahead of Dad, and Ethan always takes this climb fast. I tried to hold him in, but he managed a few good jumps. Once I looked back, and Little Missy was climbing along beside Merry Jo, digging her little feet in, as game as you please. (By this time, of course, her feet were real hooves instead of the "feathers" they had been at first.) She had never been on any kind of slope before, but she acted as if she had been climbing hills all her short life.

When we got to the top, Dad called out, "Let's stop and give our baby a chance to blow."

Her sides were going in and out, and her nostrils were wide. She was looking all around, her big eyes curious, and not a bit afraid. No doubt about it: she was going to be a very special little Morgan. And she was mine! I wanted to hug her.

We rode for about a mile. It was a beautiful day. The pines were a bright green against the sky's blue and holding up their spring candles on every branch. Spring rains had washed the air clean, and there was a wonderful smell of pine and damp earth, and horse and leather. It was good having Dad back on the trail with me again. For the past several months I had had to ride alone because of Merry Jo's pregnancy and the foal. Of course, much of that time it hadn't mattered because with the winter rains one had no urge to ride. But now, with spring really here, I could look forward to his company.

When Dad had decided we had taken Little Missy far enough for the first time out, we turned around and headed home. It was then we saw the snake. It was stretched right across the trail, a big shiny gopher snake warming its new spring skin in the afternoon sun.

Now, I don't know how you feel about snakes, but they strike horror into me. I know this is foolish, and snakes happen to be the only thing I am truly afraid of. I don't mind spiders and, like the poem, I think "Mice are nice." But snakes! I know that gopher snakes are good snakes, but I have only one speed for snakes. Good or bad, if I'm on the ground, I just take off, screaming. But now I was on Ethan, and I knew better than to scream around horses. I felt my chest tighten. I told myself that whatever Ethan might do about this snake, there was no way I was going to let him throw me!

As I've said, I was riding ahead of Dad. When I stopped, he called out, "What's the matter?"

"Don't you see it?" I demanded, pointing to the ground just ahead of me.

"Yeah, now I do. Just ride around it."

I reined Ethan to one side and moved him forward. He walked around the tail of that snake as if it had been a fallen pine branch. He couldn't have cared less. There's a real advantage in riding a horse that's been a range stallion. I breathed a sigh of relief. And the snake hadn't moved. But what would Merry Jo and Little Missy do about it? I turned in the saddle to watch them. Merry Jo arched her neck and pointed her nose at the snake, and Dad swung her wide so that Little Missy wouldn't by any chance step on it. It wouldn't have hurt her, of course, but it might have frightened her. Besides, Dad wouldn't have wanted to hurt the snake. It was a good snake; it ate ground squirrels and gophers, both of which make holes that horses can get their feet caught in and be thrown.

This trail ride with Little Missy was the first of many more, though we never again found a snake across the trail.

The trail work strengthened her flanks. She was beautifully muscled for a foal of her age. Now, at nearly six months, she stood properly, ran happily at my side around the ring, staying close to the rail as she should, and showed every sign of being ready for the show.

It had been a very happy spring, and I felt in my bones it was going to be a happy summer. School would be out in two more weeks. Mom, big as a house, had quit her job. The baby was due in August. My birthday comes in August, and I thought how nice it would be if the baby came on my birthday.

I little dreamed that disaster could be on its way to us. But it was.

7

Bad News

Everything had been going along so beautifully. Dad and I had gotten really good at housework. About all we allowed Mom to do was the cooking, and I was taking on a lot of that. I could fix vegetables, make salad and oven-fried chicken. I had even learned how to make popovers. The funny thing was that I was beginning to enjoy it. I still hated to dust, but cooking was sort of fun. I even began trying out a few recipes in Mom's cookbooks, and I came to realize the truth of what she had said to me one day: "If you know how to read, you can cook." Well, I knew how to read!

The disaster arrived in the form of a letter.

Dad had picked me up as usual at the end of our road. As usual, Diana was with me. I guess that's why he didn't say anything about the letter at first. We don't have a mailbox at our house. Dad picks up our mail at the post office.

We dropped Diana off and drove on home, and still he didn't say anything about the letter. Of course there was no reason that he should, since it was a letter to my mother from her mother.

I don't know my grandmother very well, and what I do know about her I don't like. In the first place, she doesn't like my dad, and anyone who doesn't like him can never be a friend of mine.

Her dislike of him started when he and Mom decided to get married. My grandmother didn't approve of my father as a husband for her daughter.

"You couldn't really blame her," Dad told me one day when we were out riding together in the hills.

It wasn't so very long after Missy had died, and our talk got around to old ladies, and what a great old lady Missy had been, and how different my grandmother was from her.

I don't know how to explain it, but, since we began riding together, I have felt much closer to my dad than I ever did before. And when I've been on the trail with him, he on Merry Jo and I on Ethan, the great difference between us in age sort of disappears. For one thing, on horseback I'm about as tall as he is; I can look him in the eye. And we're equal in other ways, too. If something should go wrong and Ethan got scared, there's nothing Dad could do to help me. I'm on my own, same as he is at all times. In other words, I'm not just a little kid to be protected. And when we're out alone together like on this particular day I'm speaking of, he talks to me as if I were a grown-up. So when I asked why my grandmother didn't like him and had not wanted him to marry my mother, and he had said, "You couldn't really blame her," I asked, "How come?"

I was looking across at him, and he met my eyes almost as if he were trying to decide how much to tell me.

"For one thing, I hadn't ever gone to college. For another thing, I didn't have any special trade or training. And for a third thing, I didn't have any money. Your grandmother has a lot of money, and she has a way of expecting other people to have a lot of it, too. That is, to be the right sort of people, they should have it."

"What about Abraham Lincoln?" I demanded.

Dad grinned and shook his head. "She wouldn't have liked him, either." We rode on for a bit, not saying anything, and then he spoke again. "Fortunately for me, your mother didn't share her mother's ideas. We were both young, in good health, and full of hope that everything would work out all right. We were very much in love."

"And everything *did* work out all right," I said.

"It was pretty grim at times. Especially after Martin got sick."

Martin, you may remember, was my big brother, five years older than I, who died of leukemia when he was ten years old, seven years ago.

"Your grandmother helped us then, and I've never forgotten that fact. It's the one reason I can tolerate seeing her now and then. Even though we've managed to pay it all back over the years since, still it meant a lot at the time to have her help. I'll always be grateful."

"You'd think by this time she'd forgive you and Mom for getting married when she sees how happy we all are together."

He sighed. "You'd think so. But she just can't get over wishing your mother had done better."

He didn't say anything more, and neither did I. There didn't seem to be anything more to say. But from then on, my grandmother was not one of my favorite people. I was glad that a continent separated us and that we saw each other seldom.

As I said, everything had been going along nicely. But now, with the arrival of this letter, everything was about to be changed. And not for the better.

Mom was in the kitchen when Dad and I walked in.

"A letter from your mother," he said, handing it to her.

"I've been expecting it," said Mom. "I wrote her last week about the baby coming."

"She'll be up the wall," said Dad, going straight on into the living room.

I went straight upstairs to change into my play-clothes. I didn't care one way or the other what my grandmother might think about the baby coming, and I surmised that Dad felt the same way.

Nothing more was said about the letter until we were seated at the dinner table, our food on our plates. Mom had made us kidney stew laced with wine, and Spanish rice to go with it. Next to tripe Spanish, it's my favorite dish.

"Mother will be arriving next Thursday to stay with us until the baby comes," Mom announced.

I had just taken a mouthful of rice and had to grab my water glass to wash it down before I choked and spewed rice all over the table. This horrible possibility had never occurred to me.

Dad looked calmly down the table at Mom and bit into a hard roll. "Just like that," he said.

Mom nodded. "Just like that. As you might guess, she is not happy about the baby."

"What business is it of hers?" I demanded, furious.

"Whether or not it's her business, nothing ever stopped your grandmother from expressing her opinion," said Dad as if answering my question.

"It's only natural she should want to come," said

Mom. "After all, she was with me when my other children were born. Why not this one, too? Only she isn't happy about it."

"Then she can damn well stay home!" I roared.

"*Melinda!*" cried Mom. "Don't you ever dare use such language in my presence again. What in the world's gotten into you?"

"I'll be glad to tell you." I lowered my voice some, but it shook with fury. "This is *our* baby, and the idea of someone from outside horning in on it and then not even liking it is just too much. A poor little baby not even born yet, and already there's someone who hates it. Or anyway, the idea of it, which as far as I am concerned is the same thing."

Suddenly this baby was more precious to me than anything I could even imagine. Even Little Missy.

"We've been getting along just fine," I continued, "and now this horrid old woman is crashing into our lives and changing everything." Then a bright thought hit me. "Besides, if she's mad at you it won't be good for you to have her here."

Mom laid down her fork and turned her gaze on me. "Melinda, I won't have you referring to your grandmother as a horrid old woman. It's true she doesn't see eye to eye with us. She already hates our life-style, as she calls it, and she certainly won't be very happy here. But she *is* my mother. She has done some very generous things for your father and me. She feels it her duty to come out now that I am about to have a baby, and we three *are just going to make the best of it.*"

Her last words were very emphatic, and I choked back whatever further argument I might think up.

Now Dad spoke, and his voice was carefully mild. "Don't worry, Lynn. As long as we all understand the situation, we can handle it. And it isn't as if she were going to stay forever. She *is* your mother, and I'm sure she means well. On that basis I intend to make her welcome. And I intend that you, Melinda, will make her welcome, too."

I kept my eyes on my plate and said nothing.

"Did you hear me?"

"What do you want me to do to make her welcome?" I knew my voice sounded sullen, and I didn't care.

"You are to treat her with the respect due any grandmother, and you are to remember that no matter how trying she may be, she is seventy-two years old." He glanced down the table to my mother. "What time does her plane get into Monterey?"

"Around four in the afternoon."

"Okay. I'll pick you up as usual, Melinda, and then we'll drive over Laureles grade to the airport."

It was still broad daylight by the time we had finished dinner. I decided to go down and have a talk with Diana. I *had* to talk to somebody, and Dad and Mom were not in sympathy with the way I felt. Maybe Diana would be.

So as soon as I had done the dishes, I put my head into the living room, where they were watching TV, and announced my intention.

"Get home before dark," Dad said.

I promised I would and let myself out the front door. I ran most of the way to Diana's. It's downhill all the way and quite steep, and running it is fun. A different matter when you're climbing back home again, though!

Diana let me in.

"I've got to talk to you," I said.

The familiar eager look came into her face at this hint of trouble. Diana wouldn't ever actually wish trouble on you, but she enjoys hearing about it.

"Come on into my room then," she said, turning off the TV. "Dwight's in his room cramming for a final exam, and my folks are out to dinner."

We went down the long hallway leading to the bedrooms and baths. We entered her room, and she closed the door.

Diana's room is really super. It's all carpeted and she has a canopy bed and a real desk and chair to match. She took the desk chair and motioned me into a small armchair upholstered in chintz like the drapes. The sliding glass door opened onto the patio. I could see the swimming pool glinting blue under the summer evening sky.

"Shoot," ordered Diana.

"Well, it probably doesn't sound all that terrible, but it really is. My grandmother is arriving from New York three days from now."

Diana's face registered disappointment. "What's so awful about that?"

"Because she doesn't like my dad or the idea of the baby, and I don't like her. There's bound to be trouble."

Diana took a moment to think about this. "Didn't you tell me once that your grandmother was rich?"

I nodded, wishing I had not made this boast. I couldn't remember now when I had made it or what had prompted it. But probably I had said it when Diana was bragging about something she had that we never could afford.

"Well, what's so terrible about a rich grandmother visiting you? Most people would thank their lucky stars."

"Like I said. She doesn't like my dad and the idea of the baby. That's bound to make trouble."

"I wouldn't worry too much about all that if I were you," she advised me. "Grandmothers can be very useful. As you know, I have two, and they can't do enough for me. I'm the only granddaughter. They aren't nearly as interested in their three grandsons. Dwight and my two cousins think it's gross that I'm their favorite and say that my grandmothers spoil me. My mother tries to discourage them, but I don't see anything wrong in it if they want to spoil me. Maybe your grandmother will want to spoil you, too, when she gets to know you."

Would she? Would I want her to?

"I don't think so," I replied. "She doesn't like my dad, and I'm his daughter."

"Why doesn't she like him?"

I didn't answer this right away. I wondered how much of my family's private business I should reveal, even to my best friend. Still and all, I felt as if I had to confide in someone.

"She didn't want him to marry my mother," I began, and suddenly there I was pouring out to Diana everything my father had told me that day so long ago on the trail.

When I had finished, Diana shrugged. "I don't see anything so terrible in all that. It happened a long time ago. Maybe she feels different now."

I considered this. If she had changed, then maybe Dad would change his feelings toward her. There might not be trouble, after all.

"I think I'd find it very hard to stay mad at a rich grandmother," Diana continued. "Even if she didn't like my father. Sometimes I don't like him either. Aren't there ever times when you don't like your father? Or your mother?"

I shook my head. "Not really. And I couldn't possibly like anyone who didn't like them. I don't care how rich she is."

"You're being very silly, Melinda."

I could see it was beginning to grow dark outside, and I rose from the chintz chair. "Thanks for listening, Diana, but you haven't helped much."

"I'm sorry. But honest, Melinda, give the old lady a chance. She may not be as bad as you think. And like I said, she may have changed a lot since she began not to like your dad. Think about it."

"Okay. I will."

Dwight's door was still shut when we went down the hall.

During the long steep climb back to my house, I thought over what Diana had said. Though she hadn't helped a lot, she had eased my mind a little. Maybe my grandmother *had* changed. Diana had given me a little hope. I was glad I had had a talk with her.

8

Grandmother

The big jet swooped in fifteen minutes late and taxied slowly back from the eastern end of the runway. Dad and I were waiting in the luggage section of the Monterey Airport and watched as it came up to Gate 7. The tall steps were wheeled against its side and the heavy door into the fuselage was swung open. Passengers began to descend.

"There she is," said Dad. "She's just stepping off now."

It was hard to tell at this distance just what she really looked like. Not very tall, rather chunky, carrying a large handbag with a coat flung over one arm. She wasn't wearing a hat, and her hair was pure white. There were a lot of people getting off and a lot waiting where we were. As my grandmother came through the turnstile, Dad moved toward her, a welcoming smile on his face.

"How are you, Mrs. Pryor?" I heard him say, and they shook hands warmly. Then it was my turn.

My grandmother rushed toward me and gave me a hug. She swung around to my dad. "Good heavens, but this child has grown. I wouldn't have known you, Melinda."

I wanted to say, "I wouldn't have known you, either," but it didn't seem quite right. So I didn't say anything at all.

She put a hand on my shoulder and stared hard at me. "You look just the way your mother did at your age. Twelve, isn't it?"

I nodded.

While we waited for the luggage to be unloaded, she and Dad made small talk. I listened as best I could, with all the noise going on of a hundred or more people all talking at once in a not very large space. I heard her ask after my mom and then shake her head as if it were all too much for her. If Dad noticed, he didn't pay any attention. The carts were coming in now, and he was moving up to the counter where the bags were being unloaded. My grandmother followed him, shoving ahead of several people until she stood at his elbow.

I saw her point to a large blue suitcase, then to a matching train case. Dad picked them up, and he and my grandmother came through the crowd to where I stood waiting. We followed him out to the car, and he arranged the bags in the luggage compartment. Then I climbed into the back seat, making a place for myself among the boxes that hold the mail for his route. He and my grandmother got into the front seat.

"This airport's lots bigger than the last time I saw it," said my grandmother.

"Twice as big," Dad told her.

She sighed. "A great deal can change in four years."

"It sure can around here," declared Dad. "Things don't stay the same from one season to another."

She squirmed around to look back at me. "And there are going to be some great changes in your house, Melinda."

Something mean rose up in me. "What do you mean?" I asked.

Her carefully shaped eyebrows lifted above her glasses. "What about the new baby?"

"I don't see how one little baby is going to change things very much," I said.

She gave a short laugh, the kind of laugh some grown-ups make when a kid has said something dumb.

"I think you're in for a rude awakening, my dear." She turned back to my father. "It certainly came as a surprise to me. I haven't gotten over the shock yet."

"It came as something of a surprise to us, too," Dad said, "but now that we're used to the idea, we like it."

She turned her head to face the road. "I suppose it's wise to put a good face on what you can't help."

I saw Dad's jaw muscles tighten, and I knew he was getting angry. I took heart because if they had a good fight right at the start of her visit, she might take the next plane back to New York.

"I think you'd better realize right at the start, Mrs. Pryor, that both Lynn and I will welcome this new child. And Melinda is looking forward to all the money she'll earn as a baby-sitter," he added, laughing.

This was rather loading it on, but I wasn't about to dispute him.

When we came to the place where the Carmel Valley road joins Highway One at the head of the valley and started down it, my grandmother said, "Calvin, isn't that a new condominium over there to the south across the shopping center?"

"Yes. It's been under construction for several months and it's about finished now, I believe."

"Let's drive over and take a look at it," said my grandmother.

"Sure, if you want to."

Dad pulled over into the right-hand lane for a right turn. We drove through the shopping center and approached the condominium.

"It's quite good-sized," said my grandmother. "I

imagine it will be quite attractive when it's all finished and a garden has been put in. And so convenient to the shopping center, too."

"I understand that all the apartments have been sold already," Dad told her. He laughed. "Too late for you to buy in, I'm afraid, Mrs. Pryor."

She laughed, too. "You're probably right, at that."

I didn't laugh. There was suddenly a cold spot developing in the pit of my stomach. Why had she wanted to view this condominium? Could she possibly have any ideas about living in it? But that couldn't be possible. She loved New York and thought anybody who didn't live there was disadvantaged. Gradually that cold spot began to warm up a bit. Besides, Dad had said all the condominiums had been sold. I had nothing to worry about.

She turned to me again, making conversation.

"I'm anxious to see your new house," she said.

"It isn't new. It's old. But we like it," I informed her.

"The house needs things done to it," Dad said. "We got a good buy on the property. But we have plans. When we've absorbed some of the expense of having a baby, I'm going to build on a family room. Actually, converting the back porch."

"That sounds like quite a project," said my grandmother.

"Not really," Dad told her. "The plumbing and electricity are already in. I could do it in three or four months."

"You mean you could build it yourself?" she asked in surprise.

"Sure. One of the jobs I've worked at over the past few years is carpentering." He laughed. "I even have a union card."

"Dad can do just about anything," I said.

"Now, Melinda, just because I taught you not to be afraid of horses and turned you into a good rider and built a riding ring and intend to build a family room doesn't mean I'm a jack-of-all-trades."

"You're a good mail carrier," I reminded him.

"I'd better be," he returned somewhat grimly.

My grandmother turned again to me. "Your mother has written me all about your horses."

"Did she tell you about my new foal?"

My grandmother nodded. "Yes, she did."

We turned off the valley road and started up into Toro Estates. As we approached our house, Dad said, "Here we are—last house on the road."

I kept my eyes on my grandmother as we turned into the driveway. She was looking eagerly at the house, then her eyes switched toward the barn.

"I can see your little colt, Melinda. My, isn't it cute!"

"It's not a colt; it's a filly. A colt is a male foal," I corrected her.

"Well, now, I never knew that before. You're going

to have to teach me what I don't know about horses, and that's a lot."

Dad drove across the barnyard toward the back door. We piled out of the car and Dad got out the two bags.

As we entered the back porch, Mom came out of the kitchen to meet us.

"Oh, my child," wailed my grandmother, hugging my mom to her. "How are you?"

Mom gently freed herself and stepped back, smiling. "As you see," she said.

"Lynn, *how* could you do anything so mad as to have a child at your age?"

Dad was coming along with the luggage, but he paused to hear Mom's answer to that one.

"I am exactly two years older than you were when you had me, Mother. And I was a first baby."

My grandmother had no answer for this one, and we all followed Dad into the kitchen.

"I'll take these up to your room, Mrs. Pryor."

"Thank you, Calvin. Shall I follow you up?"

We all traipsed into the front hall and followed Dad up the stairs.

"This is an interesting old house," my grandmother exclaimed as she toiled up the stairs behind Dad. "I can't wait to see all of it."

"There's not much to see," said Mom. "Six rooms; three up and three down. One front porch, one back porch, and one bath."

"Oh, dear," said my grandmother. "How do you ever manage with just one bath?"

"Quite nicely," Mom informed her. "We just try to be considerate. Our schedules are so different it's not much of a problem."

Dad led the way into the spare room. The westering sun was shining into it through the dotted Swiss curtains Mom had made for it. Its ceiling, like the one in my room, sloped cozily down over the single bed with an afghan folded at its foot. There was a bureau with a mirror hung above it. Dad had carried up the smallest upholstered chair from the living room and placed it in front of the window with our one footstool in front of it. There was a straight-backed chair against the opposite wall, and that was all the furniture. But it did look comfortable.

"Where do you want these?" asked Dad, indicating the two bags.

"Put the suitcase on the bed and the train case on the dresser. And thank you, Calvin."

"I expect you'd like to freshen up after your long trip," suggested Mom. "The bathroom is just across the hall."

We three trooped back downstairs.

My grandmother stayed upstairs for quite a while, and by the time she came down, Mom and I were well into preparing dinner. We were having roast lamb tonight—a special treat. When I went to set the table,

Mom told me to use the best table mats. When I went into the dining room, I saw that there was a new little African violet plant in the center of the table. Mom must have bought it at the supermarket where she bought the roast. We were really putting on the dog for my grandmother, and I wondered why, since nobody (except maybe my mother) really wanted her here. I thought you put your best foot forward when people were really welcome. I guess I'll never understand grown-ups.

9

Sudden Hope

When my grandmother finally did appear, she came bearing gifts. Her arms were full. There was a big package wrapped flat, which she handed to me. There were several packages, none very large, for Mom, and a long, narrow one for Dad. We unwrapped them while she chattered (my grandmother is a great talker) all about how she hadn't known just what to choose for us but hoped the gifts would prove useful. Mine turned out to be a jumper dress with two really neat blouses to go with it. The jumper was a Scotch plaid, and one of the blouses was white, and the other was exactly the same color green as was in the plaid. I liked it a lot. Mom's gift turned out to be some baby clothes and a lovely soft blanket. There was even a pair of booties. They were all white.

"I didn't know what the sex of your child was, so I decided against blue or pink," said my grandmother.

Mom looked at her in surprise. "We don't know, either," she said, and laughed.

My grandmother looked shocked. "Do you mean to say you haven't had the amniocentesis test?"

I have found out that this test tells older expectant mothers if the baby is normal, and at the same time it reveals the sex of the unborn child.

Mom shook her head. "We didn't think it was necessary since I had already had two normal children."

My grandmother sort of clucked, "Tst, tst," and shook her head, as if my mom were past all wonder. I wanted to kick her. My grandmother, I mean, not my mom. In spite of the new dress. None of this was any of her business.

Dad's gift was an expensive-looking tie.

Halfway through dinner, my grandmother turned to Dad. "If it's convenient, Calvin, I would like you to take me to a Datsun dealer next Saturday. I'm going to buy a car."

I heard Mom gasp. "Mother, that's the craziest thing I've ever heard. You're welcome to drive my VW any time you want it."

My grandmother threw up one hand as if to brush

away the very idea of driving the VW, at the same time shaking her head vigorously.

"I wouldn't *think* of driving that little bug. Besides, it's been years since I drove a gearshift car."

"For the length of time you're going to be here, Mrs. Pryor, it would be more practical, I should think, to rent a car," Dad said.

I was watching my grandmother closely. Some sixth sense warned me that there was more here than just the business of whether or not to buy a car. While I watched, I saw a new look come into her face. I don't know just how to describe it, but it had a combination of smugness and the pleasure of springing a surprise.

"The length of time I am going to be here is just the point," said my grandmother. "You see, I have made up my mind not to return to New York. I'm going to stay *right here.*"

All three of us stopped chewing to stare at her. I could feel my face freezing into an expression of horror. *She was planning to live with us.* I glanced at Dad and at Mom, who were looking down the table at each other. No one, apparently, could think of anything to say. As might be expected, it was my grandmother who spoke first. She's never silent for long.

"Well, it seems to me that one of you might say something to make me feel a little bit welcome."

Mom cleared her throat. "You've taken us by surprise, Mother. Of course we'd like to make you welcome, but as a matter of fact, I don't feel that this old house of ours is big enough to accommodate three generations."

To our further surprise, my grandmother threw back her head and laughed heartily. "You poor child! No wonder you're all looking shocked. Lynn dear, I have no intention of living with you. The fact is, I've bought a condominium here, right at the mouth of the Carmel Valley. That one near the shopping center."

"You've already *bought* it?" Dad demanded.

She nodded. "And I've given up my apartment and put all my furniture in storage. I'll be able to move in in a couple of months."

For the next few minutes Dad and Mom threw questions at her. How large was the condominium? What kind of services went with it? What was the monthly assessment? How did she arrange to buy it from New York? Et cetera, et cetera.

I said nothing. I sat there thoughtfully chewing.

So that cold spot had been a warning. She wasn't ever going back to New York. And while the three grown-ups talked about the new condominium and the details of getting all her stuff out here, I considered very carefully what the future might hold with my grandmother permanently in the picture. Because, of course, there would be no way of keeping her at arm's length, so to speak, now. You could hardly consider us a nuclear family anymore. I could see advantages, all right. She would be useful as a baby-sitter. And with a car of her own, there might be times when she could drive me places that it wouldn't be convenient for Dad and Mom to take me to. Weren't grandmothers more or less expected to spoil their grandchildren? Like Diana's two grandmothers? I never had any grandparents to spoil me. Until now. Another thought hit me. Maybe now that she was willing to live so near to him (actually only a few miles down the road), maybe she wasn't mad at my dad anymore. Again, like Diana had suggested. Maybe the years had taught her something.

Now that she was going to be a grandmother-in-residence, as it were, I began studying her with new eyes. For an old lady she was really quite pretty in a fluffy sort of way. Her hair was carefully arranged in wide waves away from her forehead. She used makeup sparingly and dressed really beautifully. She had changed out of the pantsuit she had arrived in and was now wearing a plain light-blue dress of some thin material, long-sleeved with a V neck. With it she wore a double-looped gold chain, three bangle bracelets, a gold watch, and three rings: a diamond solitaire and narrow wedding band on her left hand, and on the little finger of her right hand a rather large blue stone surrounded by small diamonds. She looked immaculately clean. And well-heeled, if you know what I mean.

I heard Mom ask a question that caught my interest.

"What made you decide to make your home out here? You're giving up a lot by leaving New York. No more great orchestras, no great drama, no great museums or universities. Aren't you going to miss all that?"

"To answer your first question first," she began, "it suddenly seemed to me ridiculous to live so far away from my children. You three are the closest people in my life, and I don't see you from one year to the next." She reached over and took my mother's hand. "I've missed you, Lynn." She looked around at Dad. "And I decided I wanted to know you better, Calvin. We haven't always seen eye to eye, but you're the closest thing to a son that I have." She looked across at me. "And then there's Melinda, my one and only grandchild. So far. I just decided I wanted to end my days among my own. Besides," she added with a kind of twinkle in her eye, "San Francisco isn't all that far away."

No one said anything for a full minute, then Dad spoke.

"I hope you won't ever regret this decision, Mrs. Pryor. But why didn't you let us know when you were first considering it instead of springing it on us this way? Not that it's any of our business, of course. It's a free world, and you have as much right to live here as we have."

"I'll tell you, Calvin. I was afraid you'd persuade

Lynn to discourage me from coming. We haven't always been the best of friends, you and I. I admit I resented you at the beginning and I hurt your pride. I've regretted that for a long time. I was wrong—I see that now. Years make a difference, and lately I've been lonely. So many of my friends are gone. I need my family now. Please let me feel I have one."

So it was as Diana had suggested. She *had* changed.

"That won't be hard to do," Dad said. "Will it, Melinda?"

He was looking pointedly at me.

"I guess not," I replied. It was the best answer I could give him at the moment.

The woman across the table was still a stranger to me. And nothing I knew about her so far had persuaded me to like her. I wondered if I could learn to like her. She seemed to want us, and that was in her favor. She had said she wanted to know Dad better. I wished I could know how he was feeling about her right now.

After dinner my grandmother insisted on helping me wash the dishes. I tried to dissuade her. I really didn't want her help. I wanted to be alone to think. Besides, I have a system. I put the dishes in the drainer and dry the pots and pans. Of course tonight, since we had had a special kind of dinner, there were more dishes than would go into the drainer all at once. But I would dry the first load and make room for the rest.

"Thank you just the same," I said to her, "but I really prefer to do them myself. I have a system."

"Dear child, I wouldn't *think* of letting you do all this work alone. Of course I'll help you."

It was no use. I opened a drawer and handed her a clean dish towel.

"You really do need a dishwasher, don't you?"

"I suppose so," I said. "We would have had one by this time, but we've been saving up for the family room."

I didn't bother to tell her that in the beginning we had been saving for a second bathroom. That was ancient history now, thanks to Diana.

My grandmother moved away from the sink and opened the door onto the back porch. She stood contemplating the porch for a moment before she spoke.

"I didn't take any special notice of this when I first arrived," she said, more to herself than to me. "Yes, I see. It would make a good family room right here off the kitchen. A good place for the baby to crawl around in. You really need this."

All at once an idea sprang at me. I was pouring the drippings from the leg of lamb into a bowl. Mom uses this for making lamb curry. I was so astonished at the idea that blazed into my mind that I slopped some of the precious juice onto the counter.

Grandmothers could be useful, Diana had said. Maybe my grandmother would get the idea of building this family room for us!

I put down the pan of drippings and crossed over to where she stood in the doorway looking at the screened porch.

"You see, the plumbing's all in," I pointed out to her. "And so's the electricity. Dad will enclose the washer and dryer, build a small powder room alongside it, and the rest of that wall will be a wardrobe closet. We'll have a spare room as well as a family room. Because, of course, our present spare room—your room—will have to become a nursery."

My grandmother nodded. "I see," she said slowly. "Yes, I see."

I began to warm to my subject. "And over on this side Dad's going to put a Franklin stove. There's plenty of room. I can have popcorn parties. He says four thousand dollars will do it nicely and leave enough over for a carpet and some furniture, too. Maybe even a deck outside with a sliding glass door onto it. I can hardly wait."

"I don't wonder," said my grandmother. "You really need this room. With the baby coming, you need it very badly." She turned back into the kitchen. "When does your father think he can get started on it?"

"Perhaps sometime next year. I'm not sure when."

She crossed to the sink and began thoughtfully to

wipe the first drainer load of dishes. She didn't say anything more about the family room. But she was looking thoughtful. Very thoughtful. Full of hope, I went to work on the second drainer load.

10

Not for Sale

June 30, 1978, fell on a Saturday, so Dad was able to get Little Missy and Merry Jo to the show and help me handle them in the ring. If it hadn't been on Saturday, I would have arranged with Dodge Rayburn, who owns the Red Barn, to help me.

The filly was in great shape now. Her coat was soft as satin and as shiny. Dad had clipped her muzzle and her ears, trimmed her hooves, and had also groomed Merry Jo within an inch of her life. Earlier we had trained Little Missy to get into the horse trailer, so we had no trouble that afternoon of the show in loading her. We put Merry Jo in first, and the filly went willingly in beside her. Mom and my grandmother were going to follow us in my grandmother's new Datsun. We had long ago entered the horses and Dad and I were wearing narrow red ribbons that said "Exhibitor." I had paid the entry fees out of my allowance savings, and I must confess I felt pretty important as we started the truck and trailer down the Carmel Valley road.

The Golden West is held at the county fairgrounds in Monterey. It is a very pretty place, with live oaks all over. From the entrance area the stalls go down in rows under the oaks to a big field where you can exercise your horses and put a last finishing touch on them.

I noticed at the beginning of one row of stalls several signs that read "Morgan Manor." This was the breeding farm owned by Mr. and Mrs. Towers. They own the great Morgan stallion, Waseeka Peter Piper, the sire of Little Missy. We drove on past, then turned down to the big field, where there were a lot of trailers parked.

It wasn't quite time for our class yet, so we took Merry Jo and the filly out of the trailer to walk them around.

Before coming down to this spot, we had stopped at the office to buy a program of the show and pick up the cards with our number on them. I looked first of all for our class in the program and noted that there were five fillies to be shown. And there, sure enough, was Little Missy's name. Owner, Melinda Ross. Our number, which we would wear pinned on our backs, was 30.

As we walked the horses around, Dad leading Merry Jo and I leading Little Missy, I noticed people looking at us.

One man finally approached us. "Isn't that Oakhill's Merry Jo?" he asked. "The one Isabel Jones used to own?"

"That's the one," said Dad.

"And that's her foal?"

"Yep."

"But she was barren. The Joneses tried to breed her time and again and never could get a foal from her. What happened?"

Dad grinned. "The woman who bought her from the Joneses found a vet who knew more than the others and"—he nodded toward Little Missy—"that's the result."

The man shook his head. "I heard that Merry Jo had had a foal, but I just didn't believe it. She's a nice-looking little filly, too."

We thanked him and continued walking around and around. Suddenly, over the loudspeaker, our class was announced, Class 55. So we started for the show ring.

I had butterflies in my stomach. I was actually going to go into a ring and show off my filly before a big grandstand full of people! Well, not exactly full, but a lot.

We joined the four other broodmares and fillies converging on the big gate where you entered the ring. As it rose in front of me, I was remembering the time two years ago when Missy had won first place in the Jack Benny. This is the event for riders thirty-nine or over. It is named for the great comedian, who, no matter how old he got, always claimed to be thirty-nine. I wished she could know that now I was here with the foal she had wanted so much and which she never saw. I looked around at the other fillies. They were dear little foals and pretty, but not one of them was as dear or, I thought, as pretty as my Little Missy.

Suddenly the gate was opened and we led our entries in. I was handling Little Missy because I had been the one who mostly had trained her and Dad was sure she would do better for me than for him.

We lined the fillies up, and the judge came over and began inspecting them, one by one. Dad and Merry Jo were right behind us, a little to one side. It was then my patient training of my filly began to show. The other four were plainly frightened at being in this big strange place. Of course, it was equally strange to Little Missy, too. Only she wasn't one bit frightened by it. Its strangeness only made her hold her head up, prick her ears forward, and look very, very alert. Which is just about the best thing that can happen to a horse which is being shown in hand. Of course, conformation is most important of all.

When the judge got to Little Missy, any stagefright I might have been feeling vanished entirely. My whole thought was of her. I had stretched her carefully as I saw him approaching and now she stood like a little statue while he walked around her.

Then he gave me the signal to trot her as he had done the others. I turned her around, saying, "Steady, girl, this is going to be fun." She gave a tiny jump, then settled into the sweetest trot you could ever imagine. We reached the turn-around spot and trotted back to the judge. I held my whip high and a bit forward to help keep her on the rail. Again she went in a straight line, picking up her feet, arching her neck, her ears pricked forward. Blood tells, and every drop in her veins was show blood. There was a little spatter of applause as we reached our starting point. I stroked Little Missy and let her relax.

Again the judge went down the line of fillies, and when he got near us, I made Little Missy stretch herself. There was another spatter of applause. She did look super!

The judge made a mark on his clipboard, crossed over to where the ring steward was waiting, and the ring steward ran across to where the announcer sat. There was a pause, and then out from the grandstand across the ring came a woman with some ribbons in her hand. She was introduced to the crowd, and then the announcer read the number of the class, its description and requirements. There was another pause, and this time, I swear, my heart stopped beating.

Then it came. "First place in Class 55 to Number 30."

My number! For a moment I couldn't move. Then I heard Dad chuckle.

"Snap out of it, Melinda. That's you!"

I whirled Little Missy around and ran her across the ring. The woman handed me a blue ribbon, and then the photographer came and took our picture. Little Missy had won a blue her first time out! And she was mine!

Dad and Merry Jo were waiting where we first started showing, because the next class was broodmare and 1978 foal. So we hadn't had to leave the ring. I had started to lead Little Missy toward them when suddenly the whole thing seemed to become too much for her. She bucked into the air, kicked as hard as she could, then started galloping toward her mother. I managed to hold onto her, but she almost pulled me off my feet. My beautifully trained, well-behaved filly was acting as badly as any foal could. A good thing she hadn't pulled this stunt while the judging was going on! I heard the announcer say over the loudspeaker, "Who's leading who?" as we came racing up to where Dad was waiting. Everyone was laughing, including him, but it was good-natured laughter, and I didn't mind a bit.

I settled Little Missy down, and then the judging of Class 56 began. Again the judge, the same one, inspected each pair, only this time we didn't have to trot them. When he had finished, Merry Jo and her foal got a third. This was fair, I thought. Because while Little Missy was without doubt the prettiest filly there, Merry Jo, for all she looked so great, was an old mare and she just didn't have the class of the two that took first and second. But she got a good hand, just the same. The crowd was showing its loyalty to the old champion who had been barren and now had the beautiful filly at her side.

When we came out the exit gate, I thought sure Mom and my grandmother would be waiting for us. But they weren't. It takes Mom a lot longer to get around these days.

However, someone was there to congratulate us. Mrs. Towers. As I've said, she's the owner of Little Missy's sire, Waseeka Peter Piper.

"Congratulations, you two," she called as we approached.

"Hello, Mrs. Towers," Dad said. "But the congratulations are all for Melinda. She's the one who has worked the filly."

"And she's done a fine job. I've been wanting to get down to see this foal ever since you told me she was here." Mrs. Towers looked very critically at Little Missy, and there was a gleam in her eye that told me she thought the filly was something special. "Let's see, she's what—six months old now?"

I nodded.

"When are you going to wean her?"

"Next month," Dad replied.

"Are you thinking of selling her?"

She had addressed the question to Dad, but it was I who replied without even thinking.

"She's not for sale," I declared firmly.

"Is that right?" The question was still directed to Dad.

"That's right if Melinda says so. It's her filly."

"I'll give you four thousand dollars for her, and that's a very fair price for a weanling in these parts."

Still I shook my head. "She's not for sale."

"With a free breeding of Merry Jo back to Pete."

Still I shook my head.

"Okay," said Mrs. Towers. "But if you ever change your mind, give me a ring, will you?"

"I'm never going to change my mind."

"But if you ever do?"

"Sure. I'll call you if I ever do."

Now Mom and my grandmother joined us. My grandmother gave me a hug and told me how proud she was of me, even before Dad could introduce her to Mrs. Towers.

Mrs. Towers smiled at Mom. "When is *your* baby due?"

"First week of August," said Mom. "I just hope it's as good-looking as Merry Jo's."

"This filly *is* exceptional," said Mrs. Towers. "She could develop into a really great mare. What are you planning to do with her, Melinda?"

I shrugged. "I don't know. I guess I'll keep working with her and in a couple of years start training her to ride."

"Don't you plan to campaign her?" Mrs. Towers sounded shocked.

"What do you mean?"

"A filly of this quality should be shown as often as possible. In another year, if she develops as I think she will, she ought to go to the Grand National at Oklahoma City. It's a crime to bottle up a Morgan like this one and use her just for riding around. She's far too good for that."

She made it sound almost as if I weren't doing the right thing by Little Missy. But I knew I was. No one could love her as much as I did, and no one would be better to her, either.

"I don't care about all that," I said. "And I don't think Little Missy does either. Anyway, she's not for sale."

The filly had been trying long enough to stand still, and she was now moving restlessly, so we said good-bye to Mrs. Towers. We started along toward our trailer down beyond the rows of stalls. Mom and my grandmother walked with us as far as the turnoff to the entrance gate and their parked car.

"What was that all about?" asked my grandmother.

"She wants to buy Little Missy," Dad said. "Offered Melinda four thousand dollars for her and a free breeding back to Waseeka Peter Piper."

I was still having my hands full with the filly, but as I listened to Dad reporting what Mrs. Towers had said, three words struck an echo in my brain. Four thousand dollars! Just the sum he had said would be needed to convert the back porch into a family room. Right here in my hand, as it were, was the thing I wanted most in the world. Before Christmas I would have a place of my own to entertain my friends. Just like Diana and the other kids. For a moment I was tempted. Besides, she had offered a free breeding back to Waseeka Peter Piper. There would be another foal.

But just at this precise moment Little Missy nudged my arm, and I turned to look at her. She came up beside me and nuzzled me the way she does, and I put my arm around her beautifully arched neck. No, not even for a family room would I part with my filly. She was too dear. I couldn't even imagine a future now that didn't hold Little Missy.

My grandmother's voice recalled me from my thoughts.

"Only four thousand dollars for a beautiful little colt like that?" (My grandmother *will* refer to the foal as a "little colt," though I have told her time and again that a colt is a male foal.) "Why, that's ridiculous. Anyway, Melinda doesn't have to sell her. And she shouldn't."

For once I was in hearty agreement with my grandmother. And though she had said nothing about it since the night we washed dishes together, she might yet come forward regarding the family room.

When we had loaded the horses and were headed home, Dad said, "We'll start weaning the filly next month, and we really ought to separate her then from Merry Jo. The way we're set up, that's pretty hard to do. No matter where we put them, those two are going to be within sight of each other, and that's going to be hard on both of them. I suggest that we put one of them down at Dodge Rayburn's barn."

"Not Little Missy!" I declared stoutly.

He shrugged. "Well, either her or Merry Jo. You'll have to decide."

How could I bear to part with the filly even for a short time? It was unthinkable. But then another thought hit me. If we put Merry Jo down at the Red Barn, Dad couldn't go out on the trail with me. That made up my mind in a hurry.

"We'll put Little Missy there," I told him. "You couldn't ride with me otherwise."

I thought he looked pleased, though he didn't say anything.

I hung the two ribbons right on each side of another ribbon already decorating one of my bedroom walls. This was the ribbon Missy had won for the Jack Benny. Her brother had come across it among her belongings after her death and had given it to me. "It really belongs to Merry Jo," he had told me, "and so it should now go to you." I thought it was very kind of him.

I stood off and looked at the three ribbons. They made a brave showing. When would I add another to them? Dad had told me that by next summer I could start competing in equitation classes in some of the small shows in our area. I would, of course, enter Little Missy in some class at the next Golden West. But at that rate, she would win only one ribbon a year. Was I unfairly bottling her up, as Mrs. Towers had said? Well, so what? There was more to enjoying a horse than collecting ribbons. I loved Little Missy, and I looked forward to training her. And when she was all grown up, it would give me terrific pleasure to know I was riding as fine a Morgan as there was anywhere around.

Little Missy was not for sale.

11

The Quarrel

It was a blistering hot afternoon. I had been down swimming in Diana's pool and was now climbing up the long road to our house. It was almost the end of July. Dad would start his three-week vacation in a few days. I knew Mom was at her doctor's for a checkup, probably her last one as the baby was due in about two weeks.

Dwight and a friend of his named Steve had been swimming with Diana and me.

Dwight has changed a lot in the past two years. Of course he has known almost from the start how I feel about him, and two years ago it sort of embarrassed him. But now that he's almost eighteen, he seems to get a kick out of it. He even goes out of his way to tease me. I don't mind a bit. I'd rather he teased me than not notice me at all.

As I came into the pool area this afternoon, he called out from the diving board, "Hi, Melinda. How's my favorite girl friend?"

I said, "Hi," and went on into the small pool house to shower and put on my bikini, which I keep here at Diana's. When I came out, Steve was sitting on the edge of the pool, his feet dangling in the water. He looked me up and down.

"Not bad," he said. "Not bad."

Dwight had completed his dive and was treading water. "Cut that out," he called to Steve, flinging his head back to get the wet hair out of his face. "I saw her first."

As I've said, I'm sort of young for my age. But not physically. I'm a big girl and well-proportioned. I could pass for fifteen, I think, in a bikini.

I could feel a sheepish grin on my face as I jumped into the water and swam past Dwight across to where Diana was floating, her arms resting on the edge of the pool.

"I heard what Steve said. You do look good in a bikini."

Diana isn't lavish with compliments, and I felt especially pleased.

"So do you," I returned.

She shook her head. "I'm too skinny."

It was the truth, but I wasn't about to tell her so. Above everything, I wanted to stay on the good side of Diana. She was, after all, Dwight's sister!

By the time I got to our house, I was so hot and sweaty I was ready to turn around and run downhill to Diana's for another swim. I crossed the lawn and entered the house by the front door. As I came into the entrance hall, I heard voices. My dad and my grandmother were in the kitchen talking. I started across the hall to the kitchen door, then paused. They weren't just talking; they were arguing. I stood still for a moment, listening. They weren't just arguing; they were quarreling.

What should I do? Should I go on in and interrupt the quarrel? I knew I shouldn't be standing here eavesdropping. I knew in my bones I should either go upstairs to my room or turn right around and go out the front door and around to the backyard so they could see me coming before I even got to the back porch. That way they could change the subject and not let me know they had been quarreling. That is what a perfectly behaved girl would do. But I am not a perfectly behaved girl. I knew I had to know what they were fighting about. In another minute I found out. They were fighting over the new family room!

"No, I won't allow you to build us a family room," I heard my father say.

"Then will you let me lend you the money to do it?

No interest, and you can pay me back when you feel like it," said my grandmother.

"And that wouldn't be giving it to us? Are you kidding? Look, Mrs. Pryor, I have said that you had as much right to live here as anyone else. That's perfectly obvious. But what you haven't got a right to do is subsidize this family. I won't have you standing around with your hand in your purse ready to pass out to Lynn what I can't afford to give her."

"Calvin, that's very unfair of you. It's all going to be Lynn's someday, anyway. Why not let her enjoy it now when she needs it?"

There was a silence, and I thought Dad was seriously considering her question. It *did* make sense in a way.

Finally he spoke. "You said the first night you were here that in years past you had hurt my pride. That's correct, you did. But I am never going to let you hurt it again."

"I understand how you feel," my grandmother said. "All I am saying is that things would be easier for Lynn if you had a family room. And it would be better for Melinda, too."

There was another long silence, which my grandmother finally broke. "We're just never going to see things eye to eye, I guess. Our backgrounds are so different. I really think—"

What she thought I'll never know because at that point Dad interrupted her.

"You're right, they're different. You're the daughter

of a judge and the widow of a corporation lawyer who died of a coronary at fifty-eight. Who worked sixteen hours a day and was absent from home a large part of the time. Lynn has told me she hardly knew her father. Well, I don't intend to be dead at fifty-eight, and I want my children to know me. I don't suppose a rural mail carrier rates very high in your list of achievements, Mrs. Pryor. But you see before you a healthy, happy man, whose wife is contented with her lot and whose daughter looks upon him as a companion and friend. It seems to me that that's quite a lot to have out of life. And I don't intend to let you come along and spoil it all by sowing discontent."

"I have no thought of doing any such thing. I was only trying to help out. But I can't help wishing sometimes that my only daughter had married someone with a bit more ambition."

My father laughed—a hard snortish laugh. "I admire your frankness, Mrs. Pryor. Now let's close this discussion and never mention the family room again. Above all, let's never let Lynn know that we've had this argument. She's been happy thinking that everything was resolved between us. I want her to go on thinking that."

I heard Dad's heavy footsteps cross the kitchen and a moment later the slam of the screen door on the back porch. I tiptoed back across the entrance hall, quietly opened the front door, and as quietly closed it after me. Then I ran around the house to the backyard as if I had just come off the road.

I was doing a lot of fast thinking as I ran. Mostly I was thinking how I hated my grandmother. Even I could tell from what I had overheard that it was true, what Dad had told me that day on our horses in the hills. She *didn't* think he was good enough for my mother. Well, my father was good enough for anybody. He was fair; he was kind; and he loved my mother and me. He never said as much, but you could just tell. I had known as soon as I was old enough to notice that my mother always came first with him. And I knew he was proud of the way I had learned to ride. He worked hard and was faithful at his job, and you could always depend on him. It made me furious that my grandmother had upset him.

Dad had almost reached the barn by the time I got around the corner of the house. "Hi," I called to him.

He stopped and waited for me to catch up with him.

"Have a good swim?" he asked.

"Super," I replied.

It was all I could do to keep from giving him a good squeeze. But this would have surprised him, since nothing had been said to prompt it. It might even have made him suspicious that I had overheard the row in the kitchen.

"What were you planning to do?" I asked.

"I thought I'd put Merry Jo in her stall and leave

Little Missy out here in the paddock for a couple of hours. They need to get used to being separated. We'll start weaning her in a couple of weeks."

"Then she goes to the Red Barn."

Dad nodded. "Right. It'll make it easier for both of them."

"I'll get Merry Jo's halter," I said. "I'll do it."

I haltered the mare to lead her into the barn. At the door she looked around, and Little Missy came running to her side. Dad had come into the paddock and was there to head her off. Merry Jo went inside reluctantly. I put her in her stall, leaving her halter on.

Out in the paddock Little Missy was nickering and kicking up a fuss. I went to her, and she butted her head against me.

"It's all right, little girl," I comforted her. "Your mama hasn't gone away. Only out of sight."

From the barn Merry Jo answered her filly's nicker.

As we were leaving the paddock, Little Missy screaming and tearing around behind us, my mother drove into the yard in my grandmother's Datsun. She hardly ever drives her VW anymore. As we walked toward her, for the first time it bothered me that she was driving a better car than my father could afford to give her. It occurred to me now that Mom didn't seem to mind a bit letting her mother do things for her. Already my grandmother had done a lot, like getting a bathing stand and a beautiful bassinet for the new baby. Would my mother let my grandmother talk her into accepting a new family room? For the first time since I had overheard the quarrel, I began to be worried. I couldn't bear to think of my father being so humiliated as to have to accept something he had already turned down. Yet if my mother really wanted it, there wasn't much he could do. Just how much influence *did* my grandmother have over her daughter? Then I remembered that years ago she hadn't had enough influence to prevent my mom from marrying my dad. Remembering, I felt a little better.

She stopped the car and called out, "What's the matter with the filly?"

"She's separated from her mother for the first time," my father said.

"Poor baby," Mom exclaimed as she awkwardly eased herself out from behind the wheel. Dad tried to help her, and she sort of fell against him. "Oh, Lord, but I'll be glad when this is over. All I need is a T-shirt with 'Goodyear' stenciled across it."

Dad laughed. "Why didn't you mention it sooner? Melinda and I would have had one made up for you."

You couldn't have told from the way he looked and talked that he had had a row with his mother-in-law a short time earlier.

My grandmother was spreading icing on a cake when we came into the kitchen. She looked up, the spreading knife in her hand.

"What did the doctor say?" she asked my mom.

"Everything's fine. He thinks the baby will arrive on time or even a little sooner. The sooner the better, I say."

My grandmother followed her across the kitchen, the knife all smeary with icing still in her hand. I happened to be right behind her, and I heard her whisper to my mother, "Did you get them?" I saw Mom nod as she gave a quick, warning look at me.

My grandmother hadn't realized I was so close, and now she made the funny face people do who have been caught doing something they shouldn't. As if they were saying, "Gosh, what have I done now?"

I knew at once, of course, that there was a secret going on between them, and to tell the truth, I didn't like it. "Did you get them?" she had asked. What could *them* be? Well, at least, it couldn't be a new family room. Could it mean plans for a new family room? Architect's plans? It didn't seem likely. I didn't think my mother would go this far without saying anything about it to my father.

In our family surprises usually happen at the dinner table. What I mean is that if somebody's going to get a present like a birthday present or a present for a special occasion, usually the "surprise" is at that person's plate at the dinner table. Mother's Day and Father's Day come on Sunday, and, of course, Easter, so these presents are at the breakfast table. But usually

120

special surprise presents appear at dinner.

So it was no surprise to me when we sat down to our dinner that evening to find a small package at my place. I was sure it had something to do with the whispering in the kitchen earlier.

"What's all this about?" I asked, the way the person being surprised always does when it's not his birthday or any other special day. "It won't be my birthday for two more weeks."

"Sometimes birthdays come a little early," said Mom, with a wink for my grandmother.

I took up the package and opened it. Lying on top of some cotton in the little box was a physician's appointment card. I picked it up, wondering. It appeared that I had an appointment to see my doctor on a certain day next week. I picked up the piece of cotton and found another small card. It said on it: "Happy birthday to a brand-new teenager from her loving grandmother." Under the card were two little gold earrings for pierced ears!

I looked across the table at my grandmother, who was looking at me with the happiest expression you could ever imagine. But as we stared at each other, I saw the happy look fade from her eyes.

"Why, Melinda, aren't you pleased?" she demanded.

I couldn't speak. I was overcome with dread. She had talked my mother into it. At the beginning of this summer vacation, at Diana's prompting, I had sounded my mother out again on the matter of pierced ears. My grandmother had been present, and I had been pleased when she backed me up. But my mother had been as firmly fixed in refusing to let me do it as she had been that first time so many months ago. Now she had obviously allowed it; my grandmother would never have gone ahead in open defiance of her. So my grandmother had talked her into it.

"Surprise has got her tongue," my father was saying, while I sat there trying not to cry.

"Aren't you pleased, dear?" my grandmother asked again.

"No," I said fiercely, and burst into tears. "Oh, *why* can't you mind your own business?"

Then I rushed away from the table and upstairs to my room, where I flung myself onto the bed and just let myself go. I think you could have heard me bawling all over Toro Estates. For now I knew with a certainty that my grandmother would talk Mom into letting her give us a family room. A family room that would be a humiliation to my father as long as he lived in this house. Oh, why had she bothered to come out here? Why couldn't she have stayed nice and far away in New York minding her own business?

I felt a hand on my shoulder. "Melinda, turn over and look at me." It was my mother. Heavy as she was, she had toiled up the stairs, and I felt a moment's shame. Then rage at my grandmother asserted itself

122

again. I turned over and sat up. "I'm truly shocked at your behavior, Melinda. How could you have so deliberately hurt your grandmother? She's completely bewildered by your conduct. She can't imagine what she has done to provoke such behavior. What *is* the matter? You *must* tell me."

I shook my head and sniffed loudly. "I can't tell you; I won't tell you. You wouldn't understand. It's about something I know she's going to make happen, and I can't bear the thought of it."

"What is this something? I'm your mother, Melinda. Surely you can confide in me."

Again I shook my head. "You're just the one I can't confide in."

"Darling, now you're hurting *me*."

It was just as she was speaking those words that my eyes, afloat with tears, happened to lift to where the horse show ribbons were hanging. For a second I stared blurrily at them while my mind began focusing on a tremendous idea. Why hadn't I thought of it sooner? How dumb could one be? Wet-faced as I was, I felt myself smiling. There on the wall hung the possible answer to my awful problem. I, Melinda Ross, could save my father's pride and make things easier for all of us. I knew now what I should do. But did I have the courage to do it?

I turned my head to look at my mother, whose face was full of concern.

"I'm sorry I said what I did downstairs, Mom. I honestly don't know what came over me to make me say it. Something's been eating at me lately. I don't want to talk about it yet. But I've just thought of something, and now everything's going to be all right. Please don't worry. I'm glad I'm going to get my ears pierced. It's nice of my grandmother to want to do it for me. It's okay, really."

My mother heaved a big sigh. "I guess at your time of life your feelings are unpredictable. But really that outburst had us all frightened. It was so exactly the opposite of what we had been expecting."

"Did Dad know about the pierced ear business?"

"Of course. You don't think I'd have let your grandmother go ahead without his consent, too?"

It was just as I had known. As long as it was all right with my mother, it would be all right with him. Datsuns, bathing tables, bassinets, earrings. Or family rooms. Of them all, only the latter was really important. Only that would be a permanent humiliation. The Datsun my grandmother would take with her when she went to her condominium in a few weeks. The bathing table and bassinet would be used only a short time and then given to some other new baby in Toro Estates. And I was bound to get my ears pierced someday. Only the family room would be there as a reminder that Mom might have married better. Well, I thought I had found a way out of that, if only I had the courage.

My mother went downstairs while I went into the bathroom to wash my face and sort of gather myself together. Then I followed her down to the dining room.

I went straight to my grandmother, put my arms firmly around her, kissed her cheek, and said, "I am truly sorry for what I said. I hope you'll forget it and forgive me. It was about something else entirely, and I don't feel that way at all now."

Turning in her chair, she returned my hug. "It's all right, dear. We all do things that surprise us now and then."

"I love the earrings, and I hope you'll go with me when I have my ears pierced."

"Of course I will if you want me."

"I really want you," I said, and returned to my seat.

It was a wonderful dinner. My grandmother had stuffed a big capon and had fixed everything that should go with it. We had the fresh-baked cake for dessert. For an old lady, and rich at that, she is a real good cook.

But the shock of what I considered doing took most of my appetite.

12

A Brave Decision

Somewhere I've read or heard that when a person is seriously hurt, like being wounded in battle, for a minute or two he feels no pain at all. He may even run a few yards before he collapses.

Well, that was more or less the way it was with me. Last night. I had felt then like a combination of Joan of Arc and the little boy with his finger in the dike. All I could think about was how good I felt about getting us a family room without my grandmother's help. I would prove that we could get along very well without her, thank you, even if my father wasn't good enough for my mother.

But when I went out to the barn next morning, what I proposed doing hit me. Really hit me. As usual, Ethan was in the ring. He nickered when he saw me, and I took hay to him and checked his water bucket. Then I started for the paddock to take care of Merry Jo and Little Missy. Merry Jo nickered as I came into the paddock, and Little Missy came bounding over, her big eyes shining, her little tail switching. In the three weeks since the show, some of her whiskers had grown out, and the inside of her ears didn't look as smooth and smart. But she was beautiful nonetheless, and until this morning I had always felt such a pride of ownership in her that my heart could hardly hold it.

This morning, though, as I put my arm around her lovely neck and felt her firm little body pressing into me, desolation swept over me. "Desolation" is the proper word. It means, according to the dictionary Missy gave me, devastation, ruin, barren wasteland, grief, sadness, loneliness. As I held Little Missy, I was feeling all those things. To add to all this, I felt as if I were about to betray this confiding little creature who, as much as any foal could, loved and trusted me. I was planning to sell her. She would be going to strangers. Worst of all, I would never see her again, except perhaps at a show now and then. And then only briefly.

I held her beautiful head up and gazed deep into her eyes. I could see my own face reflected in them. I leaned over and quickly kissed her muzzle, and she jerked it away splashed with my tears. I wondered as I stood there, with Merry Jo moving restlessly back and forth, wanting her breakfast, had anyone ever known the special kind of grief I was suffering?

Yes, someone had. I was remembering a book Missy had brought me. It was called *The Yearling*, and it was about a boy on the Florida frontier who had a pet fawn named Flag. He had loved it as I loved my filly, but when it was a year old it began to eat the family crops as they came through the soil. The family was very poor and depended on their crops, and the father ordered Jody to shoot his fawn.

I had to admit that Jody's grief was even worse than mine. He had had to kill his fawn. Little Missy wasn't about to lose her life. Like the Bible says, she would have it more abundantly. For I knew that Mr. and Mrs. Towers (they were the buyers I had in mind) would do for her what I never could. They would make her a champion, something I could never do. Shows are expensive, but even if I could have afforded to show her consistently, there was no way I could have gotten her to the shows. It would be years before I would be able to trailer her, and Dad certainly would never have the time to take her all over the state and even away off to Oklahoma City for the national Morgan show. Mr. and Mrs. Towers could and probably would. Besides, I could breed Merry Jo back. There would be another foal. This was some comfort, but my heart kept telling me that there would never be another Little Missy, and I knew my heart was right.

Still, hard as it was, saving Dad's pride was worth it.

I gave the filly and her mother an extra portion of alfalfa for having made them wait, and then gave them fresh water.

I decided to call Mrs. Towers right away and get the agony over with.

It's just about impossible to have a private conversation over the phone in our family. The phone's in the kitchen, and there's nearly always someone in the kitchen or passing through, since we seldom use the front door.

Dad was at work, and I knew my grandmother was going shopping with Diana's mother this morning. I haven't mentioned it so far, but my grandmother and Diana's mother have become quite good friends as the summer has progressed. Though there is a vast difference in their ages, they have a lot in common since they both have plenty of money and enjoy spending it. Several times my grandmother has gone down in the evening to join them at bridge. Neither my mom nor my dad play bridge, though I guess they would enjoy spending money if they had it.

So that left my mom. Should I tell her what my plan was? Could it be a secret between us? I decided against it. I knew she would try to talk me out of it. Dad would, too, if he knew. Neither of them would have wanted me to make this sacrifice for them; they knew what Little Missy meant to me.

I waited until my grandmother had driven off, and then I went to find my mother. She was upstairs in her bedroom, packing a suitcase to take to the hospital. If I had known how long she was going to stay up here, I could have chanced a call to Mrs. Towers. But if she came down in the middle of our conversation, it would be awkward, to say the least.

"Mom, can I ask a favor of you?"

"You sure can. What's on your mind?"

"I want to make a private phone call. Would you please stay up here until I finish it?"

She looked around from what she was doing, a broad smile on her face. "Now what are you and Diana cooking up?"

I smiled back. "If I wanted you to know, I wouldn't ask you to stay up here."

"Touché," she said. "I'll even shut my door."

"Thanks," I said, and hurried downstairs.

For a wonder, Mrs. Towers herself answered the phone. I had been afraid she would be out training a horse. I told her I wanted to sell her Little Missy on the terms she had offered, and she sounded very happy with my decision.

"You're really doing the wise thing, Melinda. It's a brave decision, I realize, but you're doing the best for your filly. And as a breeder, you are really contributing to the good of the Morgan breed. That's the best a breeder can hope for. I'm proud of you." Of course, I was pleased at what she was saying, though it didn't ease the ache inside me. Then she said, "Now let me talk to your father."

"He isn't here."

"Then let me talk to your mother."

"Why?"

"My dear child, I can't buy your filly without clearing it with your parents."

"But, Mrs. Towers, the filly is mine to do what I want with. You heard my father say this at the show."

"Yes, I remember his saying that, but I can't buy your filly without getting their approval *from them*."

"Okay. I'll have my dad call you about four o'clock this afternoon. Will you be home?"

She said she would be on the lookout for his call. Before we hung up, she told me again what a wise thing I was doing for the good of the filly. I listened and said nothing. I had used that argument to ease my pain, but what I was doing was for the good of my dad.

So now they would have to know. I had wanted to have the deal settled and the check in my hand before they learned about it. I guess this was foolish of me. After all, I was just a kid, even though I was almost a teenager.

I decided not to say anything until I could have my

parents together. No use having to go through it all twice.

My grandmother came home around lunchtime, and we had sandwiches. Then I saddled Ethan and headed into the hills. I wanted to put the filly as much out of my sight as possible. Ethan hadn't been out for a few days, and he was full of beans. I had to put my troubles out of my mind and start trying to think ahead of him. When we finally reached a level part of the trail, I put him into a canter, after which he settled down a lot. By the time we got home, he was pretty well lathered up, for the hot weather was holding. Dad's car was in the yard.

I sponged Ethan down, dried him off, cleaned his feet, gave him a piece of carrot, and turned him into the ring. Immediately he started rolling, plastering sand all over his nice clean, bright, shiny coat. He got up, shook himself, sending sand in all directions, then, despite the good hard ride I had given him, kicked his heels to the sky and took off in a frenzied gallop around the ring. Watching him, I felt much better than I had two hours before. No matter what, I still had Ethan, as fine a gelding as any girl could want.

The three grown-ups were all in the living room when I went into the house. I would have preferred to talk to my parents alone, but I could hardly ask my grandmother to leave the room. And I didn't think it would be courteous to ask them to come somewhere with me for a private talk. Whether I liked it or not, she was part of the family. And I knew that no matter how she felt or what she said, there was no way she was going to talk me around to letting her build the family room.

As I came into the room, they stopped what they were saying and looked at me.

"I saw you come off the trail," Dad said. "Ethan was pretty lathered up."

"He was high when we started out, so I worked him a little."

He nodded approval.

My grandmother was sitting on the sofa, and I crossed the room to sit beside her.

"I've been doing some thinking," I announced, "and I've come to an important decision."

"Hah," exclaimed my mother. "Now I'm going to learn about the mystery phone call."

"That's a part of it, all right, but not all of it. I've had this decision in mind for a long time." This was a deliberate lie, but I had to lay some groundwork. "I've decided to sell Little Missy, and Mrs. Towers is going to buy her." I looked over at Mom. "That's what the phone call was all about."

There was a long silence.

"What brought this on?" asked Dad. He didn't look happy.

"Ever since the show, I've been thinking about what

Mrs. Towers said about my bottling up the filly." I looked at Dad. "You remember when we had just come out of the ring and she was offering to buy her and telling me that I wasn't doing the best by this outstanding Morgan?"

Dad nodded.

"Well, what she said has been getting to me a lot lately. I think Little Missy deserves something better than I can give her. And after all, I can breed Merry Jo back; that's part of the deal. Of course I realize that I couldn't luck out enough to get two such fine foals in two years. The next one probably won't be as great as Little Missy. But it would still be something to train. And maybe eventually to sell."

I could feel Mom's eyes on me. I glanced over at her, and her expression was full of doubt.

She met my glance, and our eyes held.

"This sounds sort of hollow to me," she said. "I know how you love that little filly, Melinda. I can't quite understand this sudden yearning to sell her. Just what is back of all this?"

I shrugged, something I'm inclined to do when I don't have an immediate answer. I wasn't ready yet to mention the family room. One thing at a time.

"It's like I said. As she got older it would be on my conscience that I wasn't giving her a chance to be one of the best Morgan mares in the country. This is probably something only a horseman could understand," I added condescendingly.

Dad's laugh burst from him, though he tried to smother it. What I'd said did sound ridiculous, even funny. Here I was barely thirteen, with the first foal I'd ever owned, setting myself up as a horsewoman and a breeder.

"What will Mrs. Towers give you for your little colt?" asked my grandmother.

Little colt! Evidently she had forgotten what we had told her at the horse show.

"What she offered me in the first place," I answered. "Four thousand dollars and a breeding back to Pete."

"What do you plan to do with the money?"

It was the kind of question I would expect from her. I thought quickly and decided I might as well get it over with.

"It's going to build the family room."

There was a stunned silence for about three seconds, and then Mom spoke. "Oh, *no*, Melinda. We'll never let you do that."

"Why not?" I demanded with as much indignation in my voice as I could muster. "Aren't I a part of this family? Don't you think I'd like having a family room now that I am a teenager? So I can have slumber parties and fun like Diana? Besides, you'll need a place to put the baby when he starts crawling around. We *all* need this family room."

My grandmother was twitching on the sofa beside me, but for once she wasn't saying anything. I don't think she dared with Dad sitting there, his eyes looking daggers at her.

"Besides, what better could I do with the money?" I asked.

"You could put it in a fund for your college education," Mom replied.

"It'll be five years before I'm ready for college. Anything can happen in that length of time."

Only when the words were out did I realize what a ghastly prospect they might have been hinting at. I felt my face growing redder and redder. I couldn't think of a thing to say; anything would only make matters worse.

"Melinda is right," declared my grandmother. "In five years anything can happen. You need a family room now."

Mom, always the peacemaker, spoke. Her voice was carefully matter-of-fact.

"Let's not make any sudden decisions. We've been getting along very nicely so far. It'll be some time before the baby will be crawling, and your dad and I will gladly turn over the living room to you and your friends anytime you want it."

"While you two sit out in the kitchen?" I returned scornfully.

Though she didn't know it, there *was* need for haste. But I knew there was no way I could tell Mom that it would be only a matter of time, and a very short time at that, before my grandmother talked her into borrowing the money that Dad had refused.

"Yes, Mom, we do have to decide now. Next week we start weaning Little Missy. We were going to take her to the Red Barn. But if Mrs. Towers buys her, they can take her right away."

"And break your heart in the process," added Mom.

I shook my head. "Look at it this way. It's only an accident I have a filly in the first place. If Missy hadn't died, she would be owning her."

"And stabling her right here at our barn where you could enjoy her all you wanted to," Dad chimed in.

That was true, of course.

"I don't see what all this argument is about. Dad has said right along that I could do what I wanted to with my very own filly. After all, she *is* mine. Mrs. Towers is offering a fair price for her, and I have decided that it's in the best interest of Little Missy to let Morgan Manor have her. And I should think I ought to have a right to spend the money as I want to. And I want to build a family room. Now, will you please go call Mrs. Towers, Dad? She's expecting you to call her right now."

Dad rose from his chair. "I'll call her and tell her that I want you to take a little more time to think this over. I don't know how long you've had this idea about selling the filly, but my hunch is it's all very sudden. I want you to take more time to think about it."

He went into the kitchen and put in a call to Mrs. Towers. I heard him telling her that he wanted me to think about the deal a little more, but that I wouldn't sell Little Missy to anyone else in the meantime.

So okay. I would have to wait a few days, but I knew that nothing, not anything at all, was going to change my mind.

That evening when I was in bed reading, Mom came into my room. She closed the door behind her, a most unusual thing for her to do. She came straight across to my bed and sat down at the foot. Her face was very grave, and her eyes never left mine.

"Your grandmother has been talking to me."

"I'll bet."

"You can't imagine what she has proposed doing."

"Oh, yes, I can. She's offered to build the family room."

"Melinda, how on earth did you know?"

So my grandmother had ignored Dad's order not to say anything about building the family room and had gone behind his back to my mother. It didn't make me like the old lady any better.

"It just seems the natural thing for her to want to do," I said, replying to Mom's question. "She's always throwing money around."

No way was I going to let her know about my eavesdropping.

"Your grandmother is very generous. There's nothing she wouldn't do for us. She thinks it's a shame for you to sell your filly, and so do I."

"I'm selling the filly for her own good. But in any case, I don't want my grandmother giving us the family room."

"Why on earth shouldn't she if she wants to? She can easily afford it."

Should I tell her about the quarrel in the kitchen? Should I admit I had deliberately eavesdropped and then pour out to her what I had heard? I didn't think I was that kind of person. I wished now with all my heart that I hadn't listened to that conversation. Then she could have built the room as I had wanted her to do in the first place and I wouldn't have known how it had hurt my father's pride. But I had heard, and I couldn't share that fact with anyone else.

"Mom, I don't think she's changed her feelings about Dad. Not all that much anyway. And I don't think he's changed his feelings about her. Remember, she hurt his pride. She said so herself the first night she was here."

Mom nodded, looking down at the floor in front of her. "Yes, she did. She accused him of marrying me for my money. If it hadn't been for Martin, I don't think he would ever have spoken to her again. But we most desperately needed help then, and she helped us. That brought us together more or less." She turned her head to look at me and laid her hand on my legs stretched out under the light cover. "But now things are truly harmonious, Melinda. We are a family. I want to keep it that way."

"Then let me give us the family room."

"It's not necessary, dear. I'm not going to let you sacrifice your filly for a family room."

"I'm going to sell Little Missy anyway," I insisted. "My mind is made up about that. She's too good for me to keep."

"Then you can put the money toward your college education."

"Mom, if you let my grandmother give us the family room, it will hurt Dad again. *She* will be hurting him because she'll be giving us something he can't afford to give us. He has said he couldn't afford the family room and a new baby. Remember?"

"Yes, I remember. But he didn't know then that you would sell your filly and that your grandmother would want to do this for us."

"Can't you see, Mom, that he'll hate taking it from her?"

"Why on earth should he?"

Because she still thinks he isn't good enough for you, and he knows it. Because she thinks he lacks ambition, and he knows it. That's what I wanted to say but knew I couldn't.

Instead I replied, "I've already told you. She'll be giving us something he can't afford to give us. Not for a long time, anyway."

140

There was silence between us for a while, and then I said, "I'll make you a proposition, Mom. If you'll take the money I get to build the family room, I'll let my grandmother give me the money for my college education. I'll even ask her for it."

She thought this over, her eyes again on the floor.

"What's the difference between letting her help us now or later?"

"Later she'll be doing it for me, and in her crazy way I think she loves me. I'm not sure she'll ever love my father."

Mom got off the bed and started toward the door. Halfway there, she swung around. She was smiling.

"You know, my daughter, you have a lot of your grandmother in you. You're both as stubborn as mules."

I grinned. "Promise me something. Don't say anything about her offer to Dad."

"Why not?"

"He'll refuse it, and it will only upset him."

She thought a moment. "Perhaps you're right. Good night, Melinda."

I said, "Good night," and she went away.

One nice thing about the Carmel Valley, even if it's hot in the daytime, it cools off at night. As I reached over to put out my light, I could feel a cool breeze coming in at my window. I snuggled down in the bed. But it was quite a while before I could get to sleep.

13

A Way Out

This was the day Mr. and Mrs. Towers were coming for my filly. Dad had helped me groom her, clipping the inside of her ears, trimming her hooves, and putting her in show shape. I had given her a bath out under the plum tree, running a hose from Mom's washer out the back porch screen door. There was water, of course, at the barn, but it was cold water, and I wanted this last job I would ever do on her to be a good one. You can't get a horse really clean with cold water.

She looked super by the time we had finished. And she seemed very proud of herself. She pranced around at the end of her lead shank, and her tail never stopped switching. I loved her so! I wondered how I could ever bear to see her taken away from me. I had to think very hard about how important was Dad's pride. The family room didn't matter nearly so much. We would have that anyway in time. Maybe even next year. But I couldn't let my father be humiliated if there was a way to spare him that. And here, shining in the sun, was the way to do it. Little Missy.

My grandmother had been fidgeting around all morning. She came out to watch us wash the filly, then hung around while we did all the other things to her. Once when I happened to be alone, she said, "You know, Melinda, you don't have to do this."

"Do what?" I demanded.

"Sell your little colt."

"I'm doing what's best for the filly."

"I'm thinking of what's best for you."

"I need a family room—we all do."

"Of course you do"—she came right back at me—"and I can make it happen for you. Besides, I very much want to."

I shook my head. "No, you can't."

"But why?" she persisted.

"Because my father doesn't want you to."

That stopped her. She looked at me like someone who can't believe his ears.

"Where did you get that idea?"

"That's what he said."

I didn't need to tell her it was what I had overheard him say. As far as I was concerned, she could think he had confided in me. She didn't try to argue with me anymore. She went back to the house. I suppose she meant all right, only she had spoiled everything years ago, and it was too late now for her to start playing Lady Bountiful. Too late as far as my dad was concerned.

We put Little Missy in the stall and left Merry Jo out in the paddock. We had separated them several times, and they no longer fussed when they were apart. Of course they weren't apart for very long. Little Missy would stay nice and clean in the stall.

I didn't want any lunch. This was without a doubt the saddest day of my life. I would be glad when it was all over. I went up to my room, but I couldn't stay there. I didn't know what I wanted to do. I finally decided that what I wanted was to stay with Little Missy as long as possible. So I went out to the barn, got her halter, and put it on her. We had had to let it out a lot since that first time she had tried it on. She could still wear it, but it wouldn't be long before she would need a regular-size one. Morgans don't have large heads, though. Their rather short heads, wide between the eyes, with delicately molded nostrils, are one of their great attractions. Little Missy has a perfect Morgan head.

It was around two o'clock when Mr. and Mrs. Towers finally drove in. I was leading Little Missy around the barnyard. Evidently the grown-ups had seen their pickup and horse trailer cross the barnyard, for they all three came out of the house.

Everybody greeted everybody, then Mr. and Mrs. Towers began circling around the filly.

"We've bred a lot of fine fillies," Mr. Towers began, "but we've never produced one finer than this one. Wouldn't you say so, Jean?"

"She's mighty pretty," agreed Mrs. Towers.

All at once something swept over me as I stood there holding Little Missy. I couldn't bear up any longer. I could feel my face crumpling, and to spare the others the sight of it, I put my head down on the filly's back and let the tears come. Instantly Dad was at my side. I could feel his arm come around my shoulders.

"Honey, you don't have to do this. It was your own decision. Don't take it so hard. You can have another foal. And you don't *have* to sell this one."

"Yes, I do." The words came muffled from the filly's back. "I want to. It's just that it's so hard to give her up. I didn't know it would be so hard."

I could hear the others talking behind me. I knew I was embarrassing everyone, but I really couldn't help it. I reached into a pocket of my jeans and pulled out a tissue and wiped my eyes. I swallowed a last sob and turned to face Mr. and Mrs. Towers. "I'm sorry," I said.

Mrs. Towers took a step toward me, her expression deeply sympathetic. "You don't need to apologize, Melinda. We understand. And if you'd rather not sell the filly, we'll still understand."

"I do want to sell her. She's too good for me to keep. You can make her a champion. She'll be a great mare."

Now Mr. Towers spoke. "But, dear girl, you can do that for her yourself. Why can't you campaign her?"

"It costs too much, and Dad wouldn't have time to take her to shows everywhere."

"It doesn't cost as much as you may think," he said. "As for getting her to shows, you can always find people to trailer her. We trailer horses for other people all the time, and we show them. We charge a fee, of course, mostly for the trailering."

My tears were drying as I listened to him.

"I see you have a pickup and a trailer," he went on. "Often after school is out in the summer, you can find college kids who are glad to trailer horses for a reasonable wage." He smiled at me. "If that's the only reason you're parting with your filly, it's not a very good one."

He made it sound quite possible. I looked up at Dad with a question in my eyes. He smiled down at me.

"You see, you were jumping to conclusions. It looks as if you'd be able to do the right thing for the filly after all."

"I'm very sure she can," my grandmother put in.

That did it. I needed four thousand dollars, or my grandmother would surely talk my mother into accepting money from her for the family room we all wanted.

"No." I spoke sharply. "There's another reason I want to sell her. I want the money for something very important."

I saw Mr. and Mrs. Towers exchange glances.

"I've been thinking," she said into the silence that had followed my words. "In fact we discussed it on the way down here."

All eyes were on her.

"We've been thinking about your mare, Oakhill's Merry Jo. Would you sell her to us in place of the filly?"

I swear for a moment I felt the earth rock under me. This was beyond imagining. Did she really mean it?

"What—what did you say?" I knew I sounded perfectly dumb, but they were the only words I was capable of just then.

"I asked you if you would sell us Merry Jo instead of the filly. She's now a valuable broodmare, and though she's old, she could still give us several foals. Judging from this one"—she motioned toward Little Missy—"they'd more than justify what we're paying for her."

Again I looked at Dad.

"It's up to you," he said. "She's your mare."

"Yes, I'll sell her to you, Mrs. Towers."

I could part with Merry Jo. Though I loved her a lot, she had never really been my horse in the sense that Ethan was. I would always be grateful to her for Little Missy, but I could let her go to Morgan Manor. She would have a fine home.

I'd started to lead the filly toward the barn when I suddenly thought of something, and my spirits dropped again. If I sold Merry Jo, Dad wouldn't be able to ride with me anymore. I stopped and turned to Mrs. Towers.

"I've just thought of something," I told her. "I'm not sure I want to sell the mare, after all. You see, if I do, my father won't be able to ride with me anymore."

To my surprise, she laughed. "You're forgetting something, Melinda. I promised you a free breeding to Pete. His stud fee is a thousand dollars, and we have a very nice gelding we want to sell for that same price. Your dad will ride with you after all. Now let's load Merry Jo into the trailer."

We loaded Merry Jo. But not before I had kissed her soft nose and told her how much I appreciated all she had done for me. Then I got out her papers and showed them to Mr. and Mrs. Towers, and they told me what to do to change the registration of the mare from me to them. Mrs. Towers handed me a check for four thousand dollars. Then they drove away, Merry Jo riding quietly in the trailer.

I went out to the paddock where Little Missy was waiting for me. She nuzzled me, then she butted me, and then she ran off. Suddenly she stopped and looked back at me, inviting me to take after her. Of course, I did, and we raced around the paddock until I was out of breath. She was mine again! All mine! And she would be for the next thirty years. Morgans often live that long. Thirty years! I would be forty-three, older than my father was now. I walked slowly toward her. I loved her so much! She let me come up to her, and I smoothed her back and put my arms around her neck and hugged her. She was nice about it for three seconds, and I let her go. We would miss Merry Jo, Missy's dear old mare. But, oh, how super-wonderful it was to have Little Missy restored to me!

14

Gramma

Next day my grandmother took me to have my ears pierced.
She had planned to stop off first at her condominium,
as they were putting up the drapes there. After that
we were to go to the Pine Inn for lunch.

I put on the dress my mom and dad had given me
for my birthday a week ago, and I remembered to take
with me the earrings my grandmother had given me.
Also a sweater. It's always foggy and cold in Carmel
during August.

Dad waved us off. "If we aren't here when you get
back, phone the hospital," he told us.

When we had cleared our driveway and were headed

down the hill toward the valley road, my grandmother reached over and gave my knee a pat.

"Do you realize, dear, that this is the very first time we have been alone together?"

I looked across at her in some surprise. "I guess that's right. Seems sort of funny, though, when you think about it."

My grandmother is not like some women who keep looking around at their front seat passenger when they are driving. She was keeping her eyes steadily on the road and driving at the legal speed limit except when she had to slow down for a car in front of her. I have to admit that even though she is so old, she is a very good driver. Even Dad says so. So now, looking straight ahead, she said to me, "Melinda, I consider you a very bright little girl. I think you realize that there have been tensions among us since I came out here. Especially between you and me. I think we can leave your parents out of this."

I thought of the quarrel I had overheard in the kitchen. How could she leave my dad out of it? My mother, okay. But there sure was tension between her and my father. As a matter of fact, that was really the only tension there was. When it came right down to it, I couldn't think of a single disagreeable word I had ever spoken to her except that one night when I had apologized. So what did she have against me?

"What have I done?" I asked.

"Nothing that one can really put a finger on," she answered, kindly ignoring my blowup the other evening, "but you don't act natural around me. For one thing, in all these weeks, you have never addressed me by name. Not once."

Was this true? I began turning things over in my mind. It probably was, since I couldn't at the moment imagine how I would address her if I had wanted to. Would I say "grandmother"? "Grandma" sounded much too intimate for the way I felt about her. Since I couldn't decide in my own mind how I wanted to go about it, I decided to ask her.

"What do you want me to call you?"

We were driving past the Red Barn now, and I looked out to see if I could see Dodge Rayburn. Sure enough, there he was, leaning one shoulder against the big barn door and looking toward the highway across the broodmares' pasture. I waved, but I guess he didn't see me, for he didn't wave back. It's quite a distance from the road to the barn.

"On the rare occasions when I saw him, your brother always called me Gramma. Not 'Grandma' but 'Gramma.' I liked it, and I'd like it if you called me that."

"Okay," I said, "I will."

"Could you possibly say, 'I will, Gramma'?"

We had come to the electric traffic control at the entrance to the shopping center. I could feel her eyes on me, and I looked around. She was smiling, and there was a special look in her eyes. A kind of anxious look.

I smiled back. "I will, Gramma."

Just then we got a green arrow and she made her left turn into the shopping center. We drove across it to the condominium complex and parked in the carport space near her apartment.

She hadn't sent for her furniture yet. She said she wouldn't until after the baby came and she could give more time to settling when Mom was better able to take over again. There were men at work hanging drapes. It is a really neat place. There's a big living room with a dining area at one end next to the kitchen. Two bedrooms and, of course, two bathrooms.

"This will be the spare bedroom," she informed me. It was the larger of the two bedrooms. "I'm going to put twin beds in here. I expect to be having guests now and then from New York, and I sincerely hope that you and Diana will stay with me often."

"We'd like that," I said, not feeling at all sure about Diana, though I thought she might come with me at least once out of curiosity.

Our table at the Pine Inn was in a corner of the gazebo. The gazebo is a sort of glass-roofed patio. As usual, it was foggy outside, but here under the glass roof with a strong light coming through it seemed almost sunny. Terraced rows of potted flowers made it bright and cheerful.

When the waiter had taken our orders (I had the

crab casserole), my grandmother put her elbows on the table, clasped her hands in front of her and looked over the top of them at me, smiling.

"You look so exactly the way your mother did at your age—it's positively uncanny."

"What was she like?"

"A rather quiet child. Very sensible. Intelligent. I wanted everything for her. She was my only daughter and so promising."

"What were some of the things she did?"

"Oh, she went to school, and she took dancing lessons and tennis lessons and later bridge lessons. I wanted her to be adept socially. Then in the early sixties she got caught up in all the furor of that miserable time. She turned her back on all I had tried to do for her. It was her second year at college. It was then she met your father. He had been a Green Beret in Vietnam, and that made him special somehow. It was about then she decided to take up horseback riding. We were in a horsey section of Westchester County. Your father was the riding instructor at a really good academy by that time. They fell in love and eloped. I was furious, of course. I thought she had thrown herself away. My only comfort was that her father was dead and hence spared my awful disappointment."

This was all very interesting to me. I had never known how my father and mother met. Mom had never told me she had once taken riding lessons, and she had never shown any interest in riding my horses. Funny.

"How come my mother has never wanted to ride my horses?"

"That was a very painful time for all of us. She probably prefers to put it behind her. Besides, she was never really interested in riding; she was even afraid of horses. If it hadn't been for your father, she would never have gone near that academy."

"I'm glad she did," I said.

Suddenly my grandmother laughed. "So am I, Melinda. I never thought I'd ever say that. Not in my wildest imaginings. But I *am* glad. Calvin is a fine man. A good husband and a good father. You're a very happy family, and I hope I never do anything to change that." She was silent a moment, looking off across the gazebo. "I can see now that I have always been a rather managing woman. That could have ruined Lynn's life, as I look back on it. I think she would have eloped with almost anybody to get out of my clutches. Fortunately, she eloped with your father." There was another silence, then she met my eyes directly. "I don't know how much they have told you, but they haven't had an easy time of it, Melinda."

"I know."

"Things seem to be going all right now. But I must try to remember not to try to manage the Ross family."

"It wouldn't work," I told her.

"No, I can see that. My offer of the family room

was a mistake." She sighed. "If only your dad weren't so dreadfully proud."

The waiter brought our lunch, and for a while we ate in silence. All around us was the sound of pleasant chatter and the clink of glass and silver.

Finally she spoke. "It's generally conceded that grandchildren and grandparents have a special relationship. You can't even begin to understand, Melinda, how pleased I am to have a granddaughter who looks so exactly like the dear little girl I once had. It's as if Lynn had been given back to me. I hope as time goes by you'll learn to love and trust me, dear. We can have such wonderful times together if you only will."

"Diana says grandmothers can be very useful," I said. "She has two."

My grandmother, with a forkful of chef's salad halfway to her mouth, put her fork down and burst into a hearty laugh. I saw some people at a nearby table look over at us and smile.

"Diana is so right," she exclaimed. "I can see I'm going to have to be twice as useful as any single grandmother might be. But when I'm trying to be too useful, I'll depend on you to warn me."

"I'll do that, Gramma," I promised.

15

New Arrival

It hardly took ten minutes to get my ears pierced, and it hardly hurt at all. There's not much feeling in an ear-lobe. If you pinch yours real hard, you'll see what I mean. I put in the earrings, and the doctor said I had to keep them in or the holes would close. They looked real neat. I couldn't wait to show Dad and Mom.

But when we got back to the house, Dad's car was not in the yard. We rushed onto the back porch to find the kitchen door locked. Mom was gone, too! I quickly got a key out of my purse and hurried across the kitchen to the phone. The number of the Community Hospital was on a slip of paper stuck to the side of the refrigerator. When a voice answered my ringing, I said, all out of breath, "Please, do you have someone registered there by the name of Mrs. Calvin Ross? It would be very recent."

I had to wait a full minute before the same voice came on the phone again. "Sorry, we don't have that name."

I said, "Thanks," and hung up.

They must be on the way. All we could do now was wait in the hope that Dad would call us. In about thirty minutes he did. I took the call.

"Your mother is in labor, and I am going to stay here until the baby comes."

"That could be hours and hours," I said.

"They don't seem to think so," he told me. "As soon as there's any news, I'll call you."

"Is Mom—is Mom—is Mom okay?" My voice was shaky.

"She's not very comfortable right now," he said, "but she is in good spirits and everything seems to be going well."

I thought of the morning Little Missy was born and how anxious I had been that all would be well with Merry Jo. I was ten times more anxious now.

"You be sure to call," I said.

"Don't worry, honey, I will."

"Gramma and I just got home half an hour ago," I informed him.

"I'm very glad your grandmother is with you. You might just tell her that."

"I will," I promised, and we hung up.

Gramma was standing in the middle of the kitchen, waiting for my report. Her eyes were full of concern.

"Dad says everything is going all right, and he'll call us when there is any news. He also said he was glad you were with me. He said to tell you so."

She took a deep breath and let it out in a long sigh. "One feels so helpless at a time like this. Nothing we can do but wait."

"We can pray," I said.

I went up to my room to do just that. I knelt down by the window that looks across the yard to the barn and paddock. I could see Little Missy standing quietly there. I asked God to keep my mother safe and not to let her suffer more than was absolutely necessary. Then I thanked Him for letting me keep Little Missy.

I rose from my knees at last and began changing into my playclothes. I heard Gramma come upstairs and shut her door. Maybe she was praying, too. Anyway it was clear she wanted to be alone. I liked her better for it.

It was too early to feed the horses. What I wanted to do was to saddle up Ethan and take off into the hills. But I didn't want to get that far away from the phone.

I went downstairs, feeling restless. As usual, when

you really need it, there was nothing worth looking at on TV. I was glad when Gramma joined me.

"As I remember," she said, "you are to be allowed to name the new baby. What names have you chosen?"

"I've tried to think of some that are not too common. Something sort of special like Rupert or Sebastian. Then I considered Malcolm and Dudley."

"What about girls' names?"

"I haven't considered any of them because this baby will be a boy."

Gramma smiled. "What makes you so sure about that?"

"It's just got to be a boy. To make up for Martin."

She nodded. "I can understand how you could wish this. But I really think, dear, you'd better have some girls' names in reserve. Just in case," she added.

By five o'clock we still hadn't heard anything from the hospital. Well, no news was good news, I tried to tell myself. It was time to go out and feed the horses.

I threw Little Missy some hay and gathered up a big armful to take to Ethan out in the ring. He nickered as usual at sight of me, and I rubbed his poll as he dropped his lovely head to the hay. I didn't stay with him long, though, because I was too eager to get back in case the phone should ring.

Supper was sketchy. Neither one of us had any appetite. It was almost eight o'clock when the phone rang. Gramma and I were watching TV, a program on PBS. But my mind wasn't really on it, and I didn't think hers was either.

I ran to the kitchen. It was Dad.

"First off, your mother is fine." He sounded happy. "Next, you have another beautiful little filly, Melinda."

For a moment I couldn't say a thing. Then I said something utterly dumb.

"There's some mistake. It's supposed to be a boy."

Dad laughed. "There's no mistake. It's a girl, and it looks a lot like me."

I couldn't say a thing. I had never been so surprised. Or so let down. Fortunately Gramma had come into the kitchen and now was at my elbow, saying, "Let me talk to him."

I handed her the phone.

"Is everything all right, Calvin?" I heard her say. I guess everything was, because I heard her say, "Good, good," several times. They chatted for another two minutes, then she hung up.

"The baby weighs six pounds, eight ounces, is perfect, and your mother had an easy delivery. Things couldn't have gone better," she informed me. Then she laughed. "You'd better get to work on some girls' names."

"When can we see it? The baby, I mean."

"Visiting hours tomorrow morning, your father said."

"When's he coming home?"

"He said before long."

Standing there in the middle of the kitchen, I remembered to thank God for letting everything go all right. Then I began thinking about girls' names. Unusual girls' names. My mind was a blank. I couldn't even remember the names of girls in books. Then all at once a name came to me. It had come to me first in the pages of *The Morgan Magazine*, which I subscribe to. It has articles about Morgan horses, and every year one issue is devoted to Morgan mares. I remembered an article about great mares of the past which had helped to establish the Morgan breed. It mentioned particularly one mare whose name was Roxanna. *That's* what I would name the new baby. She would be Roxanna Ross, Roxy for short.

I rushed into the living room where Gramma was back to watching the program the phone call had interrupted.

"Gramma, I've got a name for the baby!"

She pressed the blab-off and looked around at me. "What is it?"

"Roxanna, and we'll call her Roxy for short. Roxy Ross. Isn't that cute?"

"A bit too cute for my taste," she said. "But it certainly is unusual."

When Dad finally drove in, we both went out onto the back porch to welcome him and get all the news as soon as possible. In the glow of the porch ceiling light, I could see he looked as beaming as I had ever seen him look. Like when I had cantered Ethan for the first time. He grabbed me and gave me a big hug and kiss. Then, to my amazement, he grabbed Gramma and did the same to her.

"What does the baby look like?" I asked.

"As I said on the phone, a lot like me."

I had forgotten.

"When can we see her?" Gramma asked, looking a little fussed at the unexpected hug and kiss. Fussed and pleased.

"Visiting hours start at ten-thirty. We'll be there then."

He didn't want anything to eat, having had something at the hospital snack bar while he was waiting for Roxy. So we all went up to bed, eager for the next morning.

It was just a little after ten-thirty when we entered the hospital. Dad led us to Mom's room. I felt terribly excited. In all my thirteen years I had never seen a really brand-new baby. Except, of course, Little Missy.

When we entered Mom's room, she was sitting up in bed, holding a small bundle in her arms.

"Hi, everybody," she greeted us. She looked happy and pretty.

We all three kissed her, then she folded back the light blanket covering the baby and I had my first look at little Roxy. Her eyes were closed, so I couldn't tell what color they were. They were very far apart, and the brows above them were dark and distinct. Clearly drawn almost as if with a pencil. Her nose was just a slight bump on her face, and her tiny mouth was perfectly shaped. There was a small dimple like Dad's in her chin. Her hair was dark and downy. Though she looked red and damp and new, even I could tell that she was beautiful.

"What do you think of your sister, daughter?" Mom asked, smiling up at me.

"She's beautiful."

"Would you like to hold her?"

"Could I?"

"Of course. Just put your two hands under her and lift her up. She doesn't weigh much."

I did as she said. And now my little sister was in my arms. She was warm and soft and cuddly. As I looked down at her, she opened her eyes and stretched her mouth in a big yawn. For a moment we gazed at each other. Could she really see me? Her eyes were dark blue and stared into mine exactly as if she were trying to figure out who I was. I squeezed her very gently, and she closed her eyes and brought her hands together, her fingers, so perfect and so tiny, crisscrossing each other in an accidental kind of way. There was a dimple like a dot at the base of each finger. Studying her, I suddenly felt a rush of love such as I had never felt before. Not even when I had held Little Missy's bony body close to me for the first time. This was my little sister, my very own, and I made up my mind then and there that I would be the best big sister any little girl ever had.

I looked over at Dad, who was watching me. "I'm glad she's ours," I said.

"I thought you might be," he replied, grinning happily.

"Do you have a name for her?" asked Mom.

"Her name is Roxanna, Roxy for short."

Mom didn't say anything for a minute. I knew she was turning the name over in her mind.

"How on earth did you ever arrive at that?" she asked.

"There was once a famous Morgan mare by that name. Troutbrook's Roxanna."

The three grown-ups burst out laughing.

Gramma spoke first. "Lynn, are you going to allow that beautiful baby to be named after a mare?"

"She could have a worse namesake," Mom said calmly. "I told Melinda some time ago that she could name the baby anything she wanted except Little Missy. I'll stick to my promise. Besides, I don't really object to Roxanna. It's unusual, and Roxy Ross is catching. I can just see it up in lights."

Gramma turned to Dad. "While we're on the subject of names and on this very happy occasion, I wonder if you and I could settle something, Calvin.

165

Could you possibly stop calling me Mrs. Pryor?"

After a moment Dad said, "On the condition that you call me Cal instead of Calvin. But what should I call you? I don't think I'd feel comfortable calling you Mildred after all these years. And I'm just afraid Mother is out, too. So what shall it be?"

"Melinda and I have come to an understanding." She looked around at me with a special comradely smile. "She has agreed to call me Gramma as Martin did. I'd be pleased if you'd do the same, Cal."

He reached out and put an arm across her shoulders and drew her toward him. "Done and done, Gramma. Nice to have it settled."

About then a nurse appeared and took Roxy to the nursery. I hated to give her up, but Mom would be coming home in a few days, and then I could hold her to my heart's content.

As I bent over Mom to say good-bye, she took my hand and held me beside the bed.

"I like your earrings, Melinda. I think they're very becoming."

As I thanked her, I felt a deep pleasure inside me. Not so much because of the earrings, though I was glad she liked them, but because it showed that even in all the excitement of having a new baby, she could still remember what was important to me. Dad hadn't once noticed them, but now Mom had, and it made me feel very good. I knew in time he would say something, too, but right now all he had eyes for were Mom and Roxy.

The first night little Roxy was home, she cried off and on all night long. We were all up dancing attendance on her, but nothing anyone did seemed to please her. Except, of course, when Mom nursed her. I guess she missed the nursery. I could see that having a brand-new baby in the house was not going to be total joy.

The next day, Friday, Gramma announced that to celebrate Roxanna's arrival she was going to take us all to brunch at Pebble Beach Lodge on this coming Sunday.

"I'd like to have Diana and her whole family come with us, including Dwight."

"Not me, thank you just the same," said Mom. "My place is here at home with Roxy for the next couple of weeks."

"I thank you, too, Gramma," said Dad, "but I think I'll just stay home with Lynn."

Gramma let out an exasperated sigh. "There goes my party. Cal, you've just got to come. There's no point in celebrating a birth without at least one of the parents present."

"Mother's right," declared Mom. "I think you should go."

"Okay, if that's the way you want it."

So Gramma went to the phone and called Diana's house. We were all in the kitchen. Roxy was asleep in a big laundry basket that Mom had fixed up as a downstairs bed for her.

I heard Gramma say, "Well, that's no problem. If Dwight has invited Steve for the day, I'd like to have him come along with us. The more the merrier."

So we were all going to brunch: Diana, her father and mother, Dwight, Steve, my grandmother, my father, and me. That made eight. I knew it would be expensive, and I was proud of that fact. And pleased that, after the number of times the Mortons had taken me to brunch, at last a member of my family was taking all of them. There was a special kind of satisfaction in it, and I felt grateful to Gramma.

For once, Sunday was a lovely day even at Pebble Beach. What fog there had been was burned off by the time we got there. The sun was bright, and beyond the wide windows of the lounge the sea was blue and white. A long line of people was passing slowly by the buffet tables, and we soon joined them.

There was just about everything you could think of to eat. We filled our plates with various kinds of fruits to start off with. Later we would return for the hot dishes: sausage, scrambled eggs, fried chicken, breakfast steak, chicken livers, you name it.

Before we started to eat, the parents raised their champagne glasses in a toast to Mom and Roxy, and we kids did the same with our fruit juice. There followed a lot of talk about Mom and the new baby, whom Diana and her family had already seen at the hospital.

They had even sent Mom flowers. More and more Diana's parents were becoming family friends and not just my friend's parents. I think Gramma has had something to do with this.

It was while we were on our second course that Diana's dad turned to mine. "I understand you're about to start on a new project, Cal."

"Yep," Dad replied. "I order the sheet rock tomorrow for the walls of the new family room. Thanks to Melinda."

He looked across the table at me and smiled.

"Thanks to Merry Jo," I corrected him.

"We're starting a new project in our family, too," Diana's dad continued. "Next month Dwight enters Stanford University."

I felt a shock wave go all through me. Dwight was going away! I wouldn't be seeing him at all. No more swims together, no more teasing. I don't know when I've felt so utterly abandoned, though I knew it was silly for me to feel so.

When I could bring my mind back to what was being said, I realized that they were talking about how expensive a college education had become. Steve said he was planning to put in his first two years at our local junior college in order to save money.

"Why don't you do that?" I asked Dwight. (I happened to be sitting next to him.) "Think of all the money you'd save."

With a sinking heart I watched him shake his head.

"I plan to enter the Stanford law school, so I think it's better to start there, too."

He was looking into my eyes as he spoke, and suddenly he grinned as he read there what was in my mind.

"Let's see now," he began, and everyone stopped talking to hear what he was about to say. "Four years at Stanford as an undergraduate, then three years of law school, and two years to settle into a practice. Nine years altogether. Will you wait nine years for me, Melinda?"

Without a moment's thought or hesitation, I said, "Oh, Dwight, I'll wait for you forever."

Everyone laughed, including Dwight, and I realized that, of course, he had been teasing. But I didn't mind. I didn't mind a bit.

Wouldn't it be wonderful if he really meant it?

About the Author

DORIS GATES was born in California and grew up not far from Carmel, where she now lives. An avid horsewoman, she enjoys riding the trails above the Carmel Valley. She has owned several Morgans and bred two Morgan foals, one of which is the model for Little Missy in this book.

Miss Gates' many well-known books include *A Morgan for Melinda*, the Newbery Honor Book *Blue Willow*, and a six-volume series of *The Greek Myths* (Viking and Puffin).

J
GAT   Gates, Doris
         A filly for Melinda

J
GAT   Gates, Doris
         A filly for Melinda

DATE	BORROWER'S NAME	
DEC 12 1985		
JUN 7 1990	1128	
DEC	1288	

HARDEMAN COUNTY PUBLIC LIBRARY
TUESDAY, WEDNESDAY 9:30 TO 5:30
THURSDAY, FRIDAY 12:30 TO 5:30
SATURDAY 9:30 TO 3:30
PHONE: 663 - 8149

© THE BAKER & TAYLOR CO.